BOUND FOR OREGON

My knees were trembling uncontrollably as I stepped on board the floating wagon. All I could think about was Daisy, our two-year-old heifer, and how she had looked in that moment when the rushing water took her away. Mother held Cynthia in her arms. Louvina, her cheeks still streaked with tears, clutched my hand as if she never would let it go. Slowly, with Father and John working hard at the oars, our lumbering craft moved out to the middle of the river. Now we were in that fast-moving current, very close to the spot where Daisy had been lost. White spray flew through the air. Beneath my feet I could feel the wagon bed being tossed and pulled. Fear moved up to my stomach, which began to churn like the swift water. I had to close my eyes.

When I opened them again, I was sure that we too were being swept away.

"Pull!" Father shouted to John. "Harder!"

I realized that now I was gripping Louvina's hand, so tight that tears were squeezing out of her eyes again.

John was paddling furiously. Father, on the downstream side, worked just as hard. The wagon creaked and groaned. It seemed as if the raging water might tear it apart.

"The appealing narrator, the forthright telling, and the concrete details of life along the Oregon Trail will draw readers into the story."   —*Booklist*

"The contrast between the tenderness of Mary Ellen's perceptions and the hardships of the frontier is deeply moving."
                                          —*Publishers Weekly*, starred review

OTHER PUFFIN BOOKS YOU MAY ENJOY

BOUND FOR OREGON

Jean Van Leeuwen

pictures by James Watling

PUFFIN BOOKS

PUFFIN BOOKS

Published by the Penguin Group

Penguin Books USA Inc., 375 Hudson Street, New York, New York 10014, U.S.A.

Penguin Books Ltd, 27 Wrights Lane, London W8 5TZ, England

Penguin Books Australia Ltd, Ringwood, Victoria, Australia

Penguin Books Canada Ltd, 10 Alcorn Avenue, Toronto, Ontario, Canada M4V 3B2

Penguin Books (N.Z.) Ltd, 182-190 Wairau Road, Auckland 10, New Zealand

Penguin Books Ltd, Registered Offices: Harmondsworth, Middlesex, England

First published in the United States of America by Dial Books for Young Readers,
a division of Penguin Books USA Inc., 1994
Published in Puffin Books, 1996

THE LIBRARY OF CONGRESS HAS CATALOGED THE DIAL EDITION AS FOLLOWS:
Van Leeuwen, Jean.
Bound for Oregon / by Jean Van Leeuwen.—1st ed. p. cm.
Summary: A fictionalized account of the journey made by nine-year-old
Mary Ellen Todd and her family from their home in Arkansas
westward over the Oregon Trail in 1852.
ISBN 0-8037-1526-9 (trade).—ISBN 0-8037-1527-7 (library)
1. Todd, Mary Ellen—Juvenile fiction.
[1. Todd, Mary Ellen—Fiction. 2. Oregon Trail—Fiction. 3. Overland journeys to
the Pacific—Fiction.] I. Title.
PZ7.V3273Bo 1994 [Fic]—dc20 93-26709 CIP AC

Puffin Books ISBN 0-14-038319-0

Printed in the United States of America

Reprinted by arrangement with Penguin Putnam Inc.
10 9 8 7 6 5 4 3 2

To Mary Ellen Todd
and all the other children
who traveled the Oregon Trail
—J.V.L.

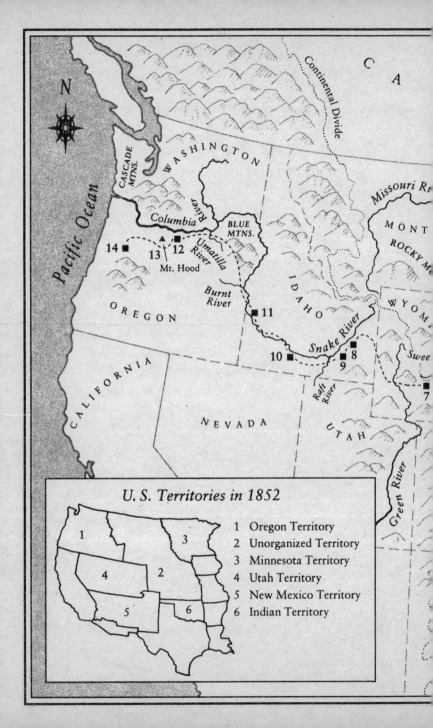

N

Continental Divide

C A

Pacific Ocean

CASCADE MTNS.

WASHINGTON

Columbia River

BLUE MTNS.

Missouri R

MONT

ROCKY M

14 ■   13 ▲ ■ 12
Mt. Hood

Umatilla River

IDAHO

WYOM

Burnt River

Snake River

Swee

11 ■

OREGON

10 ■   ■ 8
    ■ 9

Ralt River

7 ■

CALIFORNIA

NEVADA

UTAH

Green River

U.S. Territories in 1852

1 Oregon Territory
2 Unorganized Territory
3 Minnesota Territory
4 Utah Territory
5 New Mexico Territory
6 Indian Territory

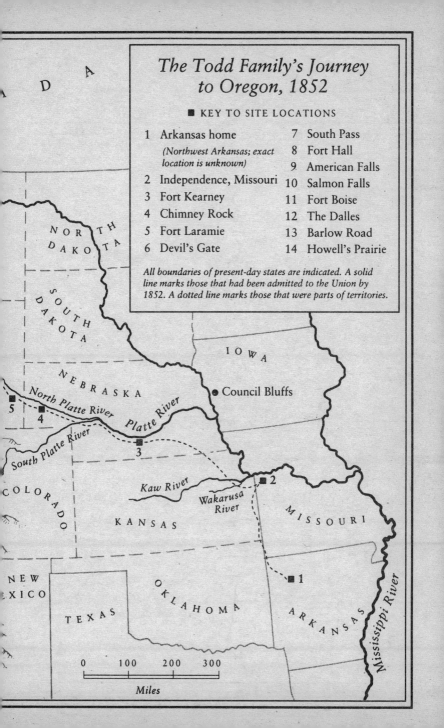

The Todd Family's Journey to Oregon, 1852

■ KEY TO SITE LOCATIONS

1 Arkansas home
   (Northwest Arkansas; exact location is unknown)
2 Independence, Missouri
3 Fort Kearney
4 Chimney Rock
5 Fort Laramie
6 Devil's Gate

7 South Pass
8 Fort Hall
9 American Falls
10 Salmon Falls
11 Fort Boise
12 The Dalles
13 Barlow Road
14 Howell's Prairie

All boundaries of present-day states are indicated. A solid line marks those that had been admitted to the Union by 1852. A dotted line marks those that were parts of territories.

CANADA

NORTH DAKOTA

SOUTH DAKOTA

NEBRASKA

IOWA

● Council Bluffs

North Platte River

Platte River

South Platte River

5

4

3

2

1

COLORADO

Kaw River

Wakarusa River

KANSAS

MISSOURI

NEW MEXICO

OKLAHOMA

TEXAS

ARKANSAS

Mississippi River

0   100   200   300

Miles

One

"Louvina, are you awake?" I whispered.

Silvery light from the full harvest moon streamed in through the curtains. My sister Louvina was curled up next to me in the bed we shared, a small, still lump beneath the bedcovers. It wasn't she who had awakened me. Was it the bright moonlight?

Then I heard voices through the thin floor below. They were talking about Oregon again.

All that fall it had been happening—ever since my father had gone to town one Saturday morning and heard a stranger talking about this marvelous country out west. Standing up on a box in the middle of the sidewalk, the man had held forth about the wonders of this western paradise: the beautiful valleys of rich black soil, the outstanding timber and water, the mild climate that could not be beaten anywhere. A farmer could take up free land out there, he said. Six hundred and forty acres of the best farmland in the world.

"And they do say, gentlemen," the man added with a smile, "that out in Oregon pigs run around under the acorn trees, round and fat and already cooked, with knives and forks sticking out of them so you can cut off a slice whenever you are hungry."

We all had laughed when we heard this, and the rest of us had forgotten about it. But not Father.

Now I could hear his voice and that of his cousin Will, along with the deep solemn voice of our neighbor down the road, George Kimball. They were talking about Indians.

I couldn't help myself. I had to know what they were saying. Usually my little sister slept so deeply that even the cannons fired off on the Fourth of July would not wake her. Just to make sure, I wormed my way over to the edge of the bed and waited a moment. Louvina did not stir.

Carefully I slid out from the warm sheets and crept to the edge of the sleeping loft. I could make out a rough triangle of the room below: the tall stone fireplace, one of the splint-bottomed easy chairs that Father had made, a pair of dust-stained boots stretched out on the hearth rug.

"Surely, Todd, you have not forgotten the Whitman massacre. Fourteen killed, including women and children. And that was only four years ago."

I could imagine our neighbor's face as he spoke, long and wrinkled and mournful-looking, like one of his old hound dogs.

"They say the Indians are quiet now," Father replied mildly.

"Ah, but for how long? The Pawnees are the worst

tribe. They will steal your horses, your stock." Mr. Kimball's voice rose, then abruptly faded so I had to strain to make it out. "Even, I hear tell, your women."

Beneath my thin nightgown a cold shiver traced its way down my backbone. *Indians. Massacres. Stealing women.* How could Father even think about making such a dangerous journey?

And why would he want to move again? I wondered. It had been less than two years since we had packed up everything we owned into a wagon and made our way from Indiana to Arkansas. Back then it was the ague that had made us move. I could still remember that sickness, with its awful chills and fever, as if I had had it yesterday.

First our bones would start to ache. Then we would grow so cold that we had to go to bed. We would lie there, shivering and shaking so hard that our teeth chattered and even the slats on the bed rattled. The next minute we would be burning up with fever. After a few days the sickness would go away, but then it would come back. Louvina and I swallowed so much bitter quinine, the taste was always in our mouths. Our relatives in Arkansas wrote to Father that they did not have the ague much there. So finally he decided to make the move. And none of us had been sick hardly a day since.

"The journey can take six months or more," Cousin Will joined in now, his thin voice filled with doubt. "Across endless plains and over the most difficult mountain ranges. It will wear out your animals."

Again Father answered quietly. "I understand the difficulties of the journey, and its dangers. But thousands are making it each year. We know how to prepare for it better than they did in the forties."

Grandma, I thought suddenly. My tiny, smiling, white-haired grandmother, who had taken care of me for six years after my own mother died, until Father married again. Only a few months ago she had come from Indiana to be near us. How could I possibly leave her again? And there was the schoolhouse just two miles down the road, with its smells of chalk and lunch pails and old wood-smoke. I loved everything about school, especially reading and committing my favorite poems to memory. And the meetinghouse, where we sang hymns each Sunday. I was partial to singing too. In that wilderness out west there would be no schoolhouses or meetinghouses, I was sure.

"Out on the plains," pronounced George Kimball in his slow, sorrowful way, "the storms are terrible. Thunder and lightning like you have never seen, hailstones as big as hens' eggs. And if you don't cross the mountains before the snows begin, blizzards will get you. You remember what happened to the Donner party."

I had overheard Father and Mother once talking about these unlucky travelers, trapped without food in the snowy mountains. They had stopped when they saw me. But from Mother's hushed voice and Father's slowly shaking head, I knew that whatever had happened to the Donner party was dreadful.

Father was silent. Surely, I thought, this meant that he was reconsidering. He would not really put his family through hardships like these. Straining to catch a glimpse of his face, I leaned over.

"Mary Ellen! What are you doing out of bed?"

It was Mother's face instead, surprised and stern, at the foot of the ladder. With her skin as white as china and her pale hair pulled back from her face, she looked ghostly in the dim light.

I knew it was useless trying to explain. Mother had her rules, and she didn't take kindly to anyone breaking them.

"Back to bed," she ordered, frowning. "Quickly now."

"Yes, ma'am," I whispered. And quick and quiet as a rabbit, I crept back to my bed.

In the morning it seemed to me I must have been dreaming. The sun shone through the curtains onto the quilt that Grandma had made for me, creamy white with a sprinkling of deep-blue stars. The smell of apples and crisp fall leaves was in the air. Next to me Louvina still slept peacefully, looking as if she had not stirred all night long. From downstairs I could hear my baby sister Cynthia laughing.

Stretching, I looked up at a tiny black spider spinning a web in the chink between logs in the corner. All that talk about Indians and snowstorms couldn't be real, I thought. This was real: our snug log house, the barn out back where Father had his pottery wheel, Mother's flower garden. And Grandma, with her smiles and hugs, just down the road. There could be no better place to live than this.

The spider, busy at its work, reminded me that it was time for our morning chores.

"Louvina." I touched her with my bare foot, and immediately her brown eyes fluttered open. It always amazed me how my sister could go from a sound sleep to wide awake in an instant. And she awoke every morning with a smile.

"Maybe if we finish our chores early, Mother will have time to work on our dresses," I told her. Mother was sewing new Sunday dresses for us out of the soft wool she spun and wove herself.

6

"Oh, do you think so?" Louvina beamed, and we both jumped quickly out of bed.

Saturday mornings were always a busy time. Mother insisted that the cabin be just so for the Sabbath. A few hours later we were nearly finished with all of the cleaning and scouring, the churning and baking. Mother was just crimping the crust of an apple pie, while Louvina watched the baby. I had only to take out the ashes swept up from the hearth and I would be free for a little while.

Stepping out the back door, I emptied the ashes into the ash hopper. We saved them for making lye, which Mother used in cooking up her homemade soap. The air was so warm for October and the sun was shining so bright, it made me feel like singing. One of the hymns I often heard at the meetinghouse on Sundays popped into my mind.

"Enter into my jaw," I sang at the top of my voice, "and sit down on my throat!"

Behind me I heard muffled laughter. I whirled around and saw John Ragsdale, the fifteen-year-old boy who did chores for Father, watching me from the woodpile.

"I think you've got your words a little mixed up," he said. He set down his axe and flashed me a teasing grin. "Don't you know it's, 'Enter into my joy and sit down on my throne'?"

John was an odd-looking boy, I thought, with his too-long arms and legs, like a knobby-kneed colt, and sandy hair that refused to lie flat on his head, and a voice that alternately squeaked and croaked. He was always teasing me. When he looked at me with his wide eyes and crooked grin, I would feel my face start to turn pink.

It was doing it now.

"Of course I knew it!" I retorted. Turning my back on him, I hurried down the path to the barn.

The barn was a world of its own, peaceful and apart. I loved its rich earthy smells, the rustlings that might be mice up in the hayloft, the stamping and shifting sounds of animals in their stalls. The minute I walked through the door, I felt safe and warm. I liked to go there after my chores were done, just to be close to the animals and to Father. Though the barn was quite large, with many stalls, we kept only three horses and about a dozen cows. That was because farming was not Father's real work. Pottery was.

I made my way down the row of stalls, stopping to give Daisy a pat. Louvina and I had named her. She was our favorite cow, a sweet-faced little two-year-old heifer the color of honey, who loved to be petted.

"Hello, Daisy." I reached my hand through the rails to her.

She looked up at me with soft brown eyes, then licked my hand all over with her rough pink tongue.

Attached to the far end of the barn was the shed where Father worked at his pottery. It smelled of damp clay and straw. I stopped in the doorway, knowing I must be careful not to disturb Father if he was at the wheel.

He was. Shoulders hunched, eyes down so he didn't notice me, he was focusing all of his attention on the lump of clay between his fingers. Father was not a tall man, but he always looked large to me when he was at his pottery wheel.

I had seen this so many times, ever since I was a tiny toddling child with Grandma holding me firmly by the hand. Yet each time it seemed new and miraculous—the

great chunk of reddish clay, the turning wheel, Father's fingers so sure and strong. Round and round spun the wheel, the clay rising, growing, changing shape until that moment when suddenly, magically, it became a jug or a milk crock or a bowl.

The moment came again. A pinch, a quick wipe of a finger, and it was finished. A pitcher this time, slender and graceful.

The wheel paused. Father looked up and smiled, and I went to sit in the straw beside him.

I knew better than to talk to him even now, as he broke off a small piece of clay and began rolling it between his hands, fashioning a handle. Instead I studied the other pitchers and jugs lined up to dry on a nearby bench. On each one, at the place where the bottom of the handle joined the vessel, I could see the clear print of Father's thumb. Looking at this thumbprint made me feel good inside. It was as if each piece of pottery he made had his picture etched into it. No matter who bought the piece or where it went, it would always somehow still be his.

The handle was smooth now, and just the right length. Working quickly, Father attached it at the top, then curled it around and pressed the end firmly into the side of the pitcher. There was his thumbprint again, as plain as could be.

I couldn't help smiling. Father smiled back. But in his gentle blue-gray eyes I could read a question. I could never keep my thoughts secret from Father for long. His eyes had a way of looking right inside my head. Without knowing I was going to say it, I suddenly blurted out, "Are we really going to Oregon?"

For a moment he didn't answer, just kept smoothing

the curve of the handle with a wet finger. Then his eyes met mine.

"I am thinking about it, Mary Ellen," he said quietly.

It was impossible to put into words the jumble of fears and regrets that swirled around inside my head. Indians and snowstorms, school, poetry, Grandma. All I could think of to say was, "But why? I like living in Arkansas. There is no ague here."

"No," Father agreed. "There is no ague here. But times are hard right now, and people are poor. They have no money even to buy one of my pitchers. Out in Oregon the land is rich and farming is easy. I have heard from people who have been there and seen it with their own eyes. And the government is giving away this rich land to anyone willing to settle it."

I could tell from the far-off look in his eyes that Father was remembering the man who had spoken in town, the one who joked about pigs with knives and forks sticking into them.

Then his face turned sober. "I know," he said, "that the journey would be long and difficult. It is more than two thousand miles, across rivers and deserts and high mountains. But many others are going. We would not be alone. And there are guidebooks now to show the way. I think that, with careful preparations, it could be done safely."

Was his mind made up, then? It almost seemed so to me.

Father's hand, rough and covered with powdery clay dust, reached out and gently brushed back the hair from my face.

"Don't worry so, Mary Ellen," he said, smiling. "Nothing has been decided yet. I must consider carefully, and

Mother and I need to talk some more. But everything will be all right, you'll see."

I nodded. As always, when Father smiled at me, it seemed as if the whole world would be all right.

Days passed. Then weeks. Still the talk of Oregon went on. Now dry brown leaves crunched beneath our feet as Louvina and I walked to school, and at night wintry winds swirled around the chimney. More friends and relatives came to sit beside the fire. Some, like young, pink-cheeked Cousin Fred and Mr. Pritchard the storekeeper, brought with them glowing letters from those who had already made the journey west. Others, like bent-over, old Great-aunt Harriet, came to offer warnings.

Father no longer whistled as he walked out to the barn in the thin gray mist of early morning. And Mother's mouth seemed permanently set in a straight line. At night, as I huddled under my star quilt and another heavier one, I could hear their low voices through the floorboards, talking and talking. It was Father, I knew, who had the Oregon fever, as people called it in town, and Mother who was not sure.

Then one evening in mid-December, just as we were finishing dinner, Father set down his knife and fork and turned to Mother.

"Well, Angelina," he said, "what do you think about our making the journey?"

My breath caught, and I put my fork down too.

Mother was silent for a moment, looking down at her plate. Her face was so still and grave that I thought I knew what her answer must be.

Then she looked up. Her chin was firm and her back

as straight as her table knife. "If others can make the journey," she said slowly, "then I guess we can too."

Father's face split into a smile, as joyful as a young boy's.

"What do you girls think?" he asked, looking across at Louvina and me.

"I want to go too!" Louvina answered right away, her short brown braids bouncing.

I opened my mouth, but no words came out. Inside my head I was hearing George Kimball's voice. "Fourteen killed . . . women and children . . . hailstones as big as hens' eggs . . ." And I was seeing Grandma's stricken face, the tears rolling down her cheeks, as we drove away from her house back in Indiana.

"Mary Ellen?" Father was looking at me intently. I could see his smile beginning to fade.

I could not bear to lose that smile.

"If you go," I said, my heart thudding in my chest, "I will go too."

Two

"Mary Ellen!" Father called. "Bring me my saw, please. And take that small bucket and get some water."

I hurried off to the well. But the minute I set down the brimming water bucket, I heard Mother's voice.

"Mary Ellen!" she called. "Will you finish this churning while I get my soap to boiling? We'll need to take a lot of soap, you know."

So much had to be done to prepare for our journey. All winter long I seemed to race from one chore to another. Churning the butter. Minding the baby. Washing dishes. Helping card and spin all the balls of soft wool that Mother wanted to take along. I hardly had any time for my lessons or for memorizing my favorite poems by Robert Burns. Of course Louvina helped too. She was six years old now, and could bring in potatoes from the root cellar and sticks of wood for kindling. And she was good at helping me watch little Cynthia.

All the time I was doing my chores, my mind buzzed

with thoughts. About leaving things behind: our comfortable house, Mother's rosebushes that she loved so much, even Father's pottery wheel, which would not fit into our wagon, he said. About school, which I might never be able to go to again once we left Arkansas. And about Grandma. Especially Grandma.

When I first told her about Oregon, stopping by her house on my way to school, Grandma had laid aside the new quilt her busy fingers were stitching on. She pulled me down into her lap, smiling. Grandma's smile was like sunshine.

"I knew your pa would come to this," she said. "I just knew it!" Behind the smile, though, I could hear sadness in her voice. "He's gone and talked himself into it. Now what am I going to do without you, honey?"

I had thought about this late into the night, and an answer had come to me. A wonderful answer.

"Oh," I told her, "you'll soon be coming to Oregon too, just as you did to Arkansas."

Grandma's thin arms tightened around me. I nestled my head into that comfortable space between her neck and soft cheek, as I had so many times before. In the silence, the ticking of the clock on the wall was like both our hearts beating.

Then Grandma gave a long sigh. "Perhaps so, child," she said softly. "Perhaps so."

She had to come, I thought afterward. I couldn't imagine being without Grandma. She had taken care of me most of the first seven years of my life. My mother had died when I was just nine months old, and Father had carried me a long, long way on horseback through the snow to Grandma's house. Everyone said I was too young to remember that journey, but sometimes I thought I did: Father's breath in the frosty air, snowflakes swirling around us, whitening the horse's dark mane, a startled rabbit hopping across our path. A few months later Father married my mother's sister. But soon after Louvina was born this wife died also. So Grandma had raised my sister and me until the time, two years ago, when he married his third wife, Angelina Tate.

As hard as I tried, I could not remember my own mother. All I knew about her was what Grandma had told me.

"She was a little bit of a thing," Grandma used to say. "No bigger than a pint of cider. But lively. Oh my, did she love to sing! And her hair was just the color of a copper penny."

I wished that I had copper-colored hair too, but mine was ordinary brown like Father's. Still, I was fond of singing.

Then there was the time when Louvina and I were playing some game and we got to laughing so we couldn't stop. All at once I noticed Grandma staring at me, tears shining in her eyes.

"What's wrong, Grandma?" I asked anxiously.

"Nothing is wrong," she answered, quickly dabbing her eyes. "It's just that you have your mother's smile."

That made two things I had of hers: her smile and her love of singing. Father never wanted to talk about my mother. It was Grandma who had given me the picture of her, hazy as it was, that I carried around in my head. Without Grandma I wouldn't have known her at all.

Father had to trade in town for a large sturdy wagon with a canvas cover and eight strong oxen to pull it. We would also need a tent for sleeping, harness, bridles, and saddles for the horses, a gun, and many tools. Then there were all the provisions for a long journey: food, clothing, medicines, extra parts for the wagon. Besides all this, Father had to make yokes and pins and bows for hitching up the oxen. And a heavy driving whip.

I watched as he filled a long slim bag, narrowed at one end, with shot. Carefully he wove narrow strips of raw-hide around it, and added a heavy handle and lashes. When he cracked it, standing outside the barn, it sounded like the shot of a gun.

"May I try it?" I asked.

But when he put the whip in my hands, with its thick handle and lashes longer than the height of a man, I could barely lift it.

Father smiled as I handed it back to him.

"It takes practice," he said.

In the meantime Mother was packing the churned butter and homemade soap into pottery jars. She wrapped other provisions in sacks or poured them into jars: flour, cornmeal, rice, beans, sugar, salt, coffee, tea, dried fruit, molasses, lard, bacon, hams. When she was not readying the food supplies, she was busy spinning and weaving strong cloth and making it up into clothing for the journey. I helped her cut out two pairs of pants for Father, and at night she sat stitching them by the fire.

"What can we take with us?" Louvina and I asked one morning.

Mother thought for a moment. "If each of you would like to make a reticule," she suggested, "you could fill them and we will try to find a corner somewhere in the wagon for them."

So Louvina and I set to work sewing two little cloth bags with drawstring tops. Inside them we put a few small toys, like our dolls with the carved wooden heads and the little pottery play dishes that Father had made. There were also compartments for needles and thread and the leftover scraps of fabric we were sewing into quilt squares. I already had ten squares finished in the Nine-Patch pattern that Grandma had taught me, and Louvina was just starting hers. And Grandma gave each of us a new thimble.

On March third, my ninth birthday, a brand-new wagon with red wheels sat outside in our front yard. Although the day was drizzly and cold, Louvina and I rushed outside to see it. The wagon looked tall and roomy, with the hickory bows that would hold the canvas cover in place curving high over the top. Father lifted us up, and the two of us sat side by side on the spring seat.

As we sat there, our journey suddenly seemed real to me. For the first time I felt a little prickle of excitement.

"We're going to Oregon," I told Louvina, cracking a pretend whip over the heads of pretend oxen. "Gee! Haw!"

Father laughed. "It won't be long now," he said.

Our departure was set for the beginning of April. Mother was worried about leaving so early, since this was the time of the worst storms out on the plains. But so many people were going west this spring of 1852, Father had heard. If we left later, there might not be enough grass for our animals to graze on. It was better to risk storms, he said, than famine.

Storms. Famine. When I heard those words, my mind clouded over again with doubts. We would be all alone out on those plains, just one small family in one wagon. Back in the fall, when Father had first spoken of going to Oregon, many others, like Cousin Fred and Mr. Pritchard, had talked about going too. But as the months went by, little by little, they had changed their minds. Of course Father said we would be safe, armed with our guidebook and a good dose of common sense, and I trusted Father completely. I wanted to do what would make him happy. Then why was it that I still felt so reluctant to leave?

Mother had a little flower garden next to the front door. Sometimes, when her critical eye decided that their colors clashed, she would dig up one or another and move it to a different spot. Some of the plants popped right out of the ground. But others seemed anchored where they were, clinging with tiny curling root fingers to their small piece of earth. Maybe I was like one of those plants, I thought, holding fast to home.

I thought of Grandma. She would not have hesitated a minute, I knew. She had married at fourteen, leaving her father's farm in Pennsylvania and going off to settle in the wilderness of Indiana. You wouldn't know it to look at her, she was so tiny and frail-looking, like a gust of wind would blow her away, but Grandma was strong. With Grandpa she had chopped down trees to build a log cabin, and in it had raised eight children. She could paddle a canoe or shoot a rifle as well as any man, she always said proudly. One time, when Grandpa was away, she shot a panther out of a tree. Another time an Indian tried to steal a ham from up in the cabin rafters.

"I was stirring a kettle of hot cornmeal mush when I saw him," said Grandma, her blue eyes dancing, when she told the story. "I just snatched up my wooden spoon out of the kettle and applied it to that Indian's backside. He left mighty quick, I can tell you."

And after Grandpa died, when she still had the five youngest to raise, Grandma had moved to town and opened up a grocery store. Oh, how I wished I was a little more like Grandma.

While I thought and worried, the preparations for our journey went on. A new bright-white canvas cover was stretched over the bows of the wagon. Then the packing began.

The wagon had high boards on its sides, making it nearly four feet deep. Father divided the space into two stories. On the bottom went everything that we would not be using every day, like the huge sacks of flour, medicines, extra clothing and dishes and wagon parts. This was carefully leveled. Then a strong piece of canvas was stretched over it, making a kind of second floor. On top of this were placed all the things that would be in daily use, neatly rolled and bundled. Father made a wooden grub box with a lid for food, and that sat in the front of the wagon, with the cooking pots wrapped snugly in sacks. An outside box was attached to the wagon for halters, hobbles, ropes, chains, axe, shovel, hammer, and other tools. And there was a rack for Father's gun.

One morning, while I was watching Father repair a harness in the barn, another of our neighbors came to speak to him. It was John Ragsdale's mother, a small faded-looking woman with a whispery voice.

"Please," she begged Father. "You must take John with you."

Father hesitated, looking at her. "I could certainly use his help with the animals," he agreed. "But are you sure?

If he goes, there is no telling when you may see him again."

I held my breath, hoping she would say yes. It wasn't surprising that John would want to go with us. We had taken him in a year ago because his stepfather was cruel to him. With six younger children to care for, including a new baby, his weary mother had nowhere else to turn. Father and Mother were fond of John, I knew, and there was something about his teasing ways that always cheered me. It would make a difference to all of us to have him along.

His mother's flushed face seemed barely able to hold in her feelings. But she nodded firmly. "He wants to go," she said.

"Then we will take him," Father promised.

Now the time was growing near. The wagon had been pulled up close to the house for the final packing. Many of our neighbors gathered around to watch. Mother kept thinking of one more thing that just had to go: a few pieces of good blue-and-white china that had belonged to her mother, some pretty tablecloths, a quart of wild plum preserves. There were the books I could not do without: Father's Bible, a volume of Robert Burns poetry and one of Longfellow, *Webster's Elementary Speller*, and a *Third Reader*, so Louvina and I could have lessons along the way. And the wooden washtub, a big brass kettle, and the rolled-up feather ticks that we would sleep on. As I handed them up one by one to Father, I thought that we were like birds building a nest.

At last Father fastened a small water keg to the side of the wagon, with a gourd dipper hanging beside it. He tied our two splint-bottomed easy chairs to the back, and hung the tar bucket for greasing the wheels underneath. We were ready to leave the following morning.

I found it hard to fall asleep that night. While Louvina sighed like a sleeping kitten in the bed beside me, I lay stiff as a log, my eyes staring up into the darkness. All sorts of strange visions danced around in my brain. Painted Indian faces turned into Grandma's face, tears streaming down her cheeks. Hens' eggs fell out of the sky, changed into snow, and piled up in our wagon. But despite all my fears I knew that nothing could keep us from making this journey now. Finally, with the words "we're going to Oregon, we're going to Oregon" repeating over and over in my ears, I fell into an exhausted sleep.

Then suddenly it was morning, a bright sunny spring day, and Mother was calling us.

"Mary Ellen! Louvina! Come and help."

We hurried through breakfast. I helped Mother pack up our lunch in a basket. Then Louvina and I went outside to hand up the last of the cooking pots and our quilts and feather pillows to Father. Mother was busy sweeping out the empty house, to leave it tidy for the family to whom we had sold it. Meanwhile relatives and friends were arriving to say good-bye.

"Go and ask Mother if she has anything else to go in the wagon," Father told me.

I walked in the open door. Mother had finished sweeping, and the straw broom leaned against the wall next to the fireplace. That and a bare china cupboard that was too heavy to take with us were the only things left in a room that had always seemed crowded with furnishings. I looked at the fireplace, neatly swept out now, and the places where our two easy chairs had sat. The outline of the hearth rug still showed on the dark plank floor, worn smooth by the tread of many feet. The room felt strange to me, empty and cold.

Mother appeared, taking off her apron.

"Father wants to know if there is anything else for the wagon," I said.

"Just these." Mother held up a wooden spoon and a folded paper of her flower seeds.

For a moment, neither of us moved. I stared around the room, trying to memorize it, not as it looked now but as it used to be. Though Mother said nothing, I thought maybe she was doing the same.

"Well," she said finally, "Father is waiting."

Our footsteps made a hollow sound as we walked to the door. I didn't look back when Mother latched it.

Father had sent John to gather up the animals. There were the four pairs of oxen, two milk cows named Lillie and Blackie, and our tame little heifer, Daisy. Louvina and I begged Father to take her along, and at last he had agreed. Then there were Father's two horses, Polly and Pet, and our watchdog, Rover.

The oxen were soon hitched to the wagon, and Polly was saddled for John to ride. Father stood next to the team, his new whip ready in his hand. Still, he did not give the order to move out.

We were being wrapped in hugs, covered with kisses, passed from one pair of arms to another. Cousin Fred nearly squeezed my breath away. Then came Cousin Martha and the minister's wife and Great-aunt Harriet.

"You'll be a good girl, won't you, Mary Ellen?" she whispered in my ear. "And take care of your little sisters."

"Oh, I just know we will never see you again!" someone wailed.

Cousin Will tickled me with his beard, then passed me to Mrs. Pritchard, who enfolded me in her plump arms.

"Keep up your courage," I heard the tall, pale young minister saying to Mother. "And whatever happens, don't fret. Courage will do more for you than anything else."

John's mother and younger sisters hovered over him. Even George Kimball, as worried-looking as ever, was giving Father some last-minute warning.

Finally I came to Grandma.

"Oh, honey, honey!" was all she could say to me, her bright blue eyes shining.

"Remember," I told her fiercely, wrapping my arms around her waist. "You'll soon be coming to Oregon too."

Grandma did not answer, just held me close for a long time. And I felt tears falling on my hair.

Slowly we climbed into the wagon, underneath that clean, white canvas cover. Mother was crying softly. Louvina and Cynthia looked scared. Finally, Father popped his whip.

"Gee, Buck!" he shouted.

The wheels began to turn, and the oxen moved toward the road.

Looking back through the round gathered opening in the wagon cover, I saw all the familiar faces, some smiling, some tearful, the many waving hands. Grandma, leaning on Cousin Will's arm, looked small and forlorn, her handkerchief clutched in one hand, the breeze ruffling her wisps of white hair. Suddenly I was filled with the most overwhelming sadness. Maybe it was true, I thought. Maybe we would never see any of those faces again. Not even Grandma's.

My eyes blurred with tears, and I couldn't help it. I put down my head and cried.

When I finally was able to look back again, the faces had disappeared from sight. All I could see was the rutted dirt road, the pale-green budding trees, and Rover, his white plume of a tail waving, running alongside the wagon.

The wheels rattled and creaked.

"Going-to-Oregon," they seemed to say. "Going-to-Oregon."

Three

That night for the first time we ate our dinner around a campfire. Mother brought out the good baked chicken that John's mother had cooked for us and the salt-rising bread and sweet cake that Grandma had made. The evening air was warm. Newly awakened frogs sang a cheeping song from a nearby creek. The wagon cover gleamed in the firelight. Rover lay curled between Louvina and me, his ears alert as always, his head pressing against my knee.

In spite of his warmth, I felt a little shiver of loneliness. It seemed strange to be outside beneath the dark sky and towering trees instead of inside our snug house. The sky, with its faraway pinpoints of stars, was so vast and we were so small. Louvina seemed to feel it too. She was quiet, and Cynthia, who rarely sat still, rested sleepily in Mother's arms. John stared silently into the fire. Had he been missing his family, I wondered, as he ate his mother's chicken with the propped-up lid of the grub box for a table and an ox bow for a chair? Was he wishing now that he had never asked to go along?

Then all at once Father began to sing in his deep, clear voice. It was one of the hymns that we often sang at the meetinghouse on Sunday mornings: "My Faith Looks Up to Thee." After a minute Mother joined in, then John, in his uncertain cracking voice, and then Louvina and I. As the last notes died away, Father said quietly, "You know, God is just as near to us here as He is at home."

Leaning back on his elbows, he gazed up into the starry sky.

"Look, girls," he said, pointing. "There is Sirius, the brightest star in the heavens. And near it, do you see four stars close together? That is Orion, the Hunter."

"I see it!" cried Louvina excitedly. "I see the brightest star."

As I looked where Father's finger was pointing, it seemed to me that the stars had moved closer. And that they were watching over us.

A few minutes later John left us to make up his bed in the tent. We changed into our nightclothes and climbed into our own strange new beds inside the wagon. It was crowded, with trunks and barrels and the big washtub hemming us in, Louvina's elbow poking into my back, and everyone's breathing all mixed up together. But it felt snug.

"Good night, girls," came Father's soft, muffled voice. "Sleep well."

I pulled Grandma's quilt close around me, thinking of her fingers darting in and out, making all the hundreds of tiny stitches that held it together.

"Good night," I answered.

The last thing I saw before I closed my eyes was a sprinkling of stars shining through the round opening of the wagon cover.

When I awoke the next morning, I smelled bacon frying. Father had already made a fire and gone with John to milk the cows. Mother was cooking breakfast, baking biscuits in the black iron Dutch oven set over the fire.

"You can get dressed," she told me, "and then help your sisters get ready for breakfast. Quickly now! We want to make an early start."

After breakfast I washed the tin dishes while Louvina minded Cynthia. Mother strained milk, put up lunches for noon, and packed everything back into the wagon. Father and John pulled down the tent pole and carefully folded the tent. Then they yoked up the oxen, and once more we were on our way.

The wagon rolled along, rocking and creaking. Father walked ahead, next to the team, while John drove the animals behind. Mother sat up on the spring seat, her back straight as always, her face shaded by her green lace-trimmed sunbonnet. Cynthia was next to her in the small padded box that Father had made, just big enough for her to play and sleep in. Louvina and I rode inside the wagon, the cover tied up at the sides so we could see out. The cool breeze riffled through our hair.

For a while we played with our dolls, dressing and undressing them with scraps of fabric. Louvina could entertain herself this way for hours, but after a little while I grew restless. I hated sitting still. The oxen plodded so slowly. And there was nothing new to see, just the same winding road and new-green trees, dotted here and there with bursting blossoms, and small streams and an occasional cabin, its chimney sending up a thin ribbon of smoke into the cloudless blue sky.

Then I made a discovery. If I stepped out onto the brake block, I could jump down to the ground without the wagon stopping.

This was a good game, I thought.

"Louvina, watch this!" I called, climbing up to try it again.

Mother turned around to look at me. "Be careful of the wheels," she warned.

"I will be."

I jumped free of them easily. But my heel caught in the hem of my blue, flower-sprigged dress, and I heard a harsh ripping sound.

It was only a tiny tear, I could see right away. Still, I could feel Mother frowning as I got quickly to my feet. She was always reminding me to be a lady. Why was that so important? I wondered. Why was it that most of the activities I thought were fun, like running and jumping and climbing, were not considered ladylike? Sometimes I found myself wishing that I had been born a boy. Then I could have fun and not worry about skirts constantly in my way.

It felt good to stretch my legs. I waved to John and he waved back, grinning. I walked along next to the wagon, stopping occasionally to pick an early spring flower or watch a bee buzzing in the grass or play a game of fetch with Rover. If the wagon got too far ahead, all I had to do was say, "Come on, Rover!" And we ran for a few minutes to catch up.

When we finally stopped late that afternoon, Father said, "We have come about twelve miles today, and Mary

Ellen must have walked six of them." He smiled at me. "If you keep that up, you will walk halfway to Oregon."

But after the third day the weather turned showery. Mother, who hated a mess, would not let me climb in and out of the wagon with my muddy shoes. So I had to spend all my time inside. Though I found it hard to sit still, Louvina and I thought of ways to amuse ourselves. We made up new games with our dolls and with a yarn ball that Mother had brought along. We read our books. We sang all the songs we could remember. "Happy Day" was our favorite, and we sang it the loudest when it was raining the hardest. We brought Cynthia in back with us and tried to teach her new words.

"Gee! Whoa! Haw!" she cried to the oxen in her tiny voice, making us laugh.

Sometimes John rode up alongside the wagon, his long legs dangling down over Polly's round sides.

"Hi thar, Cynthia!" he would call in his high-pitched voice.

"Hi thar, Don!" she would answer in the exact same voice, and even Mother had to smile.

Most nights we slept in the wagon, with John nearby in the tent. But once in a while toward twilight, when the setting sun stole the warmth from the sky, we would come upon a farmhouse or a log cabin in the woods, and we would be invited to spend the night. It felt good to eat dinner on a real table in front of a blazing fireplace and sleep in real beds again.

At these stops everyone was anxious to know where we were going. When Father told them, they all seemed to have advice to offer.

"Once you reach the wild prairies, you don't want to

be traveling alone," cautioned one farmer, whose long solemn face reminded me of George Kimball. "You still have over two thousand miles of wilderness to go, you know. Your best bet is to wait in Independence for a wagon train to be made up and join with it."

I had heard Father and Mother debating this several times late at night, as I lay wrapped up in the quilt Grandma had made. It was a question, it seemed, of making faster time or of having the protection of a large wagon train.

Now Father set down his steaming coffee cup, looking straight at Mother across the table.

"That is what we aim to do," he answered. And Mother smiled.

We crossed into Kansas and headed north along the border toward Independence, Missouri. By now we were growing used to traveling in the wagon. We were up each morning at sunrise and, after a quick breakfast, were on our way by seven. When the sun climbed high in the sky, Father would choose a shady place for nooning, an hour to rest and eat our lunch and let the cattle graze. After that we moved on again until late in the afternoon, when we made camp. Except for the wagon bogging down in mudholes after a rain, the traveling was fairly easy. We had not seen a single Indian, nor had we encountered any of the severe spring storms that Mother worried about. Most days we made twelve to fifteen miles.

Father and Mother could now pack up the wagon in a few minutes' time. John, who no longer showed any sign of being homesick, was becoming an experienced hand with the animals. Mother was learning to bake good sourdough bread. And I was able to wash the dishes faster every day. We found that if we hung a covered bucket of milk under the wagon each morning, the turning of the wheels acted like a churn, and by evening a nice little pat of butter would be floating on top.

As the days grew warmer, Mother insisted that Louvina and I wear sunbonnets and long mitts to protect our faces and hands from the sun. Louvina obeyed cheerfully. She always did what she was told. She was so good, with her round pretty face and her happy smile. Her eyes were like windows that you could look through and see inside her head. And inside she was good too, sweet-natured and truthful and kind.

But I was different. I hated the feeling of that long bonnet poking out over my face and kept finding excuses to take it off.

Once again I saw Mother frowning at me.

"Do you want to look like that, Mary Ellen?" she asked, pointing out two girls with freckled, sunburned faces walking along the road.

Secretly, I didn't care if I did. Having a pale complexion was just another bothersome part of being a lady, it seemed to me. A picture suddenly flitted across my mind of a mother with copper-colored hair, a little bit of a thing, happy and busy like Grandma, a mother who never frowned.

"No, ma'am," I answered reluctantly.

After a while I got used to wearing my sunbonnet, but I never stopped hating it.

Although it was important to keep moving, Father and Mother did not feel it was right to travel on the Sabbath. So on Sundays we would rest for at least part of the day. Our animals grazed on the abundant, soft green grass.

Father took down his rifle and went hunting for rabbits and squirrels and quail. Mother brought out the big brass kettle to heat up water, and the washtub became a bathtub. After we bathed, she would prepare a special big Sunday dinner, with pie made from dried apples for dessert. Afterward I sometimes took walks with Father, and he would tell me about all the rocks and trees, plants and birds and insects that we saw. One time I found a petrified clam shell. And we would read and sing and study the Bible. I liked to commit whole chapters to memory. My favorite was the Twenty-third Psalm, because it reminded me of our journey.

> *The Lord is my shepherd; I shall not want.*
> *He maketh me to lie down in green pastures:*
> *He leadeth me beside the still waters.*
> *He restoreth my soul . . .*

We had been traveling more than three weeks now and had come close to three hundred miles.

"In another day or two we will be in Independence," Father said.

That night, as I lay under my warm quilt, listening to a few drops of rain pattering lightly on the wagon cover over my head, I wondered what it would be like being part of a wagon train. There would be other children to play with, I knew. And we had been told that sometimes there was fiddle music and young people dancing around the campfires in the evenings. I thought I probably would like camping with other families.

Thunder grumbled in the distance. Lightning flickered. I could hear the wind starting to rise.

Then all at once there was a clap of thunder louder than any I had ever heard. It seemed to come from somewhere deep inside the earth, rumbling and shaking, filling the space between earth and sky with a noise that would never end.

Moments later the rains came. Huge raindrops pelted down, peppering the wagon cover. Within a few minutes the sides were all soaked through. Our bedclothes were wet. Our nightclothes were wet. Cynthia was crying in an awful, high wailing voice. Mother was trying to comfort her. Louvina and I huddled close together to keep warm.

"It's all right," Father's calm voice reassured us. "It is only a storm. It will soon be over."

"Over now!" sobbed Cynthia.

But the wind whistled and shrieked, and the thunder kept crashing. This was the kind of storm George Kimball had warned us about, I thought, and all my fears came rushing back. With each thunderclap I could feel the wagon tremble. I was sure that at any moment the cover would be torn off, and our wagon would capsize.

Wrapping my quilt tight around me, I thought of Grandma. How I longed for her loving arms around me, her soft voice giving me courage. Father was busy trying to fasten down the wagon cover. Mother was too distracted by Cynthia's crying to have time for me. Besides, she never had been one for hugging and kissing. All at once I thought of the time when I was very little, maybe two or three, and Grandma took me with her to Uncle Jimmie's store. Uncle Jimmie put me in an empty maple sugar barrel, and I sat inside it for a long time, eating all the little sugar lumps stuck to the sides. When I cried to get out, he sat me up on the high counter, grinning at me with his laughing eyes and black curly hair. "Is that little girl for sale?" someone asked. And Grandma came and swooped me down into her arms and said, "Never!"

I felt a choking in my throat and tried to hold back my tears, pulling the damp quilt over my head so no one would hear.

"It's all right," Father's soothing voice came again. "The wind is beginning to die down. It is nearly over."

The wind moaned and the rain dripped. Thunder rumbled, moving slowly away until it was only a faint mutter in the distance. I was so tired that at last I fell asleep.

Four

Never had I seen so many wagons and tents, or the smoke of so many campfires. From my favorite perch up on the spring seat of our wagon, they stretched out as far as I could see. And more families were arriving in Independence every day, Father said. I wondered how they would ever find an unoccupied spot to make camp.

Father had made arrangements for us to travel in a large train of a hundred wagons. In just three or four days we would be starting out. The men had met to choose a captain and other officers, and had written out rules to make the journey together easier. In the meantime everyone was busy replenishing food supplies in the bustling shops of Independence, trading for the strongest oxen and mules, making last-minute repairs on wagons, giving the wheels a final greasing so they would roll along smoothly.

"My land," said Mother, shaking her head at all the noise. "This surely is a lively place."

I had to agree. Many families were traveling in large

groups, with three or four wagons and drivers hired on to herd their cattle. All day long hammers banged and saws buzzed, dogs barked and cattle bawled. Children were everywhere, racing around campfires, jumping over wagon tongues, tripping over tent pegs. Some of the men were rough-looking and quarrelsome, and Mother warned us to stay away from them. Every day there were dogfights, and sometimes fistfights. It was so different from our peaceful evenings with just our family around the campfire. But I liked the excitement.

Next to our wagon was a family named Grant, who had a son, David, about John's age. Within hours we had all become fast friends. John and David rode off together to drive the cattle to pasture. Mother and Mrs. Grant were comparing pie recipes, while Father and Mr. Grant worked to repair a broken wheel on the Grants' wagon. I had a way sometimes of thinking of people as animals, and Mr. Grant put me in mind of a strutting red rooster in a barnyard. He was a little man who walked like a big man, chest puffed out, full of smiles and talk and elaborate plans. His wife, thin and nervous as a bedraggled hen, looked as if she was worn out trying to keep up with him.

"Where are you from?" Mother asked her that first day.

"Most recently, from Illinois," Mrs. Grant answered. "But I was born in Massachusetts."

It turned out that they had lived in five states, but never long in any one, as Mr. Grant was too restless to stay put. Each move had brought them farther west. But this one, Mrs. Grant claimed, was going to be their last.

"You can't go farther west than the Pacific," she said, with a smile that seemed a little sad to me.

Nearby was another family with two children just the same ages as Louvina and me. I played games of "Annie Over" with red-headed laughing Charlie and a bunch of other boys, one team on either side of his wagon. We tossed a ball over, and whoever caught it would run around the wagon and try to tag one of the other team. If you were tagged, you had to join that team. The game went on, full of running and shouting, laughing and arguing, until everyone was on the same side. And Louvina had Charlie's little sister, Matilda, to play dolls and other quiet games.

When Mother called us, Louvina would return to the wagon as neat and tidy as when she had left, while I came back all rumpled and dirty, my dress covered with dark grass stains. It seemed as if Mother was constantly frowning at me.

My real mother wouldn't care about a few grass stains, I thought, scowling. Inside my head I could see her again, little and lively and smiling, sunlight glinting on her bright copper hair.

In another camp was an old grandmother, not like Grandma at all, but wrinkled and shriveled-looking, who always had a pipe in her mouth. I had to pass her wagon every time I went to fetch water for Mother.

"Howdy, sis," she would say to me in a cracked high voice. "What be your name?"

"Mary Ellen Todd," I would answer.

She would stare at me, her pipe bobbing slowly up and down. "You do be a fine little gal," she told me.

And the next time I passed by on my way to fetch water, she would say exactly the same thing.

Also in a wagon near us was a girl named Lucinda,

who had been very sick for a long time. I had never seen her, because she could not come outside except on the warmest days. But her mother told Mother that the family was making the journey west in hopes of curing her.

One morning Mother used the last of her eggs to make a boiled custard.

"Perhaps Lucinda would like some," she said to me. "Would you take over a cup?"

Hesitantly I approached her family's wagon. I did not know what a very sick girl would look like.

"Lucinda?" I called softly.

A hand reached out and pulled aside the wagon flap, and I could see inside. Sitting on a mattress, a gray wool shawl draped around her shoulders, was a dark-haired girl with a thin delicate face. Her mother sat next to her, combing out her long hair.

"My mother thought you might like some custard," I said, holding out the cup.

Slowly the girl turned her head, looking at me with large brown eyes. Her face was as white as the wagon cover, the skin covering it nearly transparent, as if you might see inside to blood and bone. She reminded me of something, but I couldn't quite remember what.

"Thank you very much," she said in a light musical voice.

A butterfly, I thought, as I hurried away. That was what she reminded me of: a frail, fluttering white butterfly.

I went to look for Charlie. Suddenly I felt the urge to run and jump and play loud shouting games.

The best times in camp were the evenings. Campfires burned cheerily in the darkness, and everyone would gather around them. The men told stories, long and rambling and punctuated with deep bursts of laughter, while the women knitted or sewed in the half-light. Some of the camps had fiddles or flutes or banjos, and music seemed always in the air. Louvina and I played games of hide-and-seek with Charlie and Matilda and the other children until Mother found us and sent us to bed. Afterward I lay listening to the sound of a nearby fiddle—gay rollicking melodies that could change unexpectedly to a slow sorrowful tune that brought tears to my eyes—until finally I fell asleep.

The day before we were to start out I was helping Father grease and tar the wagon wheels. We had removed one wheel to work on it. Mother was baking biscuits in the Dutch oven over the fire, while Louvina and Cynthia played quietly inside the tent.

Suddenly behind me I heard a low, rumbling growl. I turned around to see a big red hound dog about to jump on Rover.

Rover growled back.

"No, Rover!" I tried to warn him. The red dog was twice his size, his legs and powerful neck scarred from fighting.

But Rover paid no attention. In a moment the two dogs were rolling around in the dirt, furiously snapping and snarling. First one was on top, then the other, in a tangle of red and white fur. Poor Rover was bound to get the worst of it. How could I save him? I wondered.

I could not even get near him. Now the tumbling dogs bumped against the side of the tent, knocking over a bucket of water. It spilled on Cynthia, and she began to wail.

"There, there, Cynthia," soothed Mother. "It's all

right." Jumping up to go to her, she dropped the lid of the Dutch oven, spilling coals all over her biscuits.

In his hurry to help, Father stumbled over the wagon wheel and fell almost on top of the snarling dogs. I jumped up on the brake block to get out of the way. Cynthia and Louvina were both sobbing with fright now, as the dogs rolled toward the fire.

Just then a long, stringy-looking man in homespun breeches and a limp brown hat came hurrying toward us. He had a straggly beard and squinting eyes, and his mouth was sunken in, as if he had lost all his teeth.

"Towser!" he cried, aiming a hard kick at his dog's ribs. "Be gone with you, you scamp!"

The big red dog slunk quickly away, and Rover crept under the wagon to lick his wounds.

The man peered at him, then at Father. Hands on hips, chewing on a huge wad of tobacco, he ambled toward the fire.

"That Towser's a mighty fine dog," he drawled, a sly grin playing around the corners of his mouth.

I knew what that grin meant. It was daring Father to contradict him. Father was a peaceable man who never looked for an argument. Still, this was how many of the fistfights in camp got started.

I watched Father's face, waiting for his reply. He was frowning at the ground, his jaw tightly clenched.

"I reckon," he said quietly.

The man swaggered up close to the fire, then spit out a stream of tobacco juice right next to Mother's biscuits.

I heard her gasp. Mother never let anyone, even us children, near her cooking fires. All at once I noticed a circle of faces just beyond the campfire. A crowd of men and boys was gathering, as if sensing a fight about to start. I held my breath, waiting to see what would happen.

There was a long moment of silence. Very slowly Father bent down, brushed the ashes from the biscuits with his fingers, and covered them with the lid of the Dutch oven. Then, getting to his feet, he looked the man steadily in the eye.

"Looks like it might be going to rain again," he observed, as calmly as if he were talking to the family at dinner.

The man took a step back and looked up at the sky.

"I wouldn't wonder," he agreed gruffly.

Reaching into his pocket, he took out a plug of tobacco and a knife. Slowly and deliberately he cut off a large corner and stuffed it into his cheek.

"Well," he mumbled, "I guess I might as well be goin'."

"Good day to you," said Father, still staring at him.

"You too, sir," the man replied. And he ambled away, still chewing for all he was worth.

I let out a long breath of relief. Like fog, the crowd quickly melted away. As soon as everyone was gone, Rover came limping out from under the wagon. His long white fur was matted, and blood ran from cuts on his foot and one black ear. Louvina and I threw our arms around him, and he licked our faces as if to say he was sorry.

Father lifted Cynthia, still wet and scared, into his arms.

"Don't yike big doggies!" she kept whimpering over and over.

"You girls were all very brave," Mother told us, kneeling down to tend to her biscuits.

Although she did not often show us affection, I had

to admit that when we did something right, she always said so.

She looked up at Father. "Well," she said, puffing out her cheeks and imitating Towser's master's voice, "I guess I might as well be goin'."

And they both smiled.

Father had been the brave one, I thought, as I went to refill the water bucket. Yet it was puzzling. Nothing had really happened, just a few words around a campfire. It was not so much what Father had done but what he hadn't done—been drawn into a fight—that seemed brave to me.

Later, as we ate our evening meal of biscuits, fried bacon, potatoes, and apple dumplings around our grub-box table, we told John the story of the dogfight.

"W-what?" he stammered in surprise. "Rover was attacked by Towser? Why, I'd have thought that big old pot hound would chaw him up just like his master chaws tobacco!"

Rover, hearing his name, wagged his tail happily. And we all had a good laugh.

Five

"Come, Buck."

Father spoke quietly, holding up the yoke. Obediently the big brown ox stepped into his place next to Ben. Father pinned the bow with expert hands, and the eight oxen were ready to be hitched to the wagon.

Mother was busy wrapping up the kettle and frying pan and stowing them with the rest of the breakfast things in the grub box. All around us I could see other families pulling down tents and heaving boxes into wagons. Mothers were calling to children in impatient voices. Horses were being saddled and cattle rounded up. Some oxen, not as well-trained as ours, protested loudly as drivers struggled to put the yoke on them.

Father took out his big pocket watch.

"Six-fifty," he announced. "It's nearly time."

Mother scooped up Cynthia from where she was crouched looking at ants in the grass and climbed up on the spring seat. Louvina and I took our places just behind her. I wanted to be sure to be able to see everything.

A moment later the captain blew a loud blast on his silver trumpet. Whips cracked and drivers shouted. For a few minutes the wagons milled around in seeming confusion. Then slowly they began to string out in an orderly line, facing west.

We were on our way.

To me it was a beautiful sight: the line of white-covered wagons stretching out in front of us, the moving wave of cattle, the riders sitting tall and straight on their horses. And Father's whip curling over the heads of our oxen as he shouted, "Gee, Buck! Gee, Ben!"

Soon we crossed over the border from Missouri into Kansas. We were out on the wild prairie. In all my imaginings I had never dreamed that there could be so much space, wide and flat and empty. The sky seemed bigger here, like an enormous bright-blue lid set down over the earth. Green-gold grass waved on every side, bobbing and nodding in the constant wind. Yellow-chested larks flew up from their nests on the ground as we passed by. Here and there the grass was dotted with spring flowers, pink and purple, yellow and blue. I breathed in their perfume as I walked along. Though I had never seen an ocean, these great shimmering waves of grass reminded me of what one must be like. They rippled and rolled, up small hills and down, and on and on as far in front of us and behind as I could see.

Traveling in a large wagon train was much different than traveling alone, we soon found out. There was all the dust raised by so many feet and turning wheels. The dust was worst when the wind blew, and especially for those unlucky families at the rear of the train. Because of this a rule was made that the wagon in the lead one day had to drop all the way back the next, giving everyone an equal turn. It seemed to me too that we moved more slowly—so slowly that Mother, who never would allow her hands to be idle, was able to do her mending as we moved along. And the grass for grazing now had to be shared by hundreds of animals, so ours could not do as well.

In spite of these drawbacks, though, I liked being part of a wagon train. There was always something interesting to watch, Charlie and Matilda to play with, and music and once in a while even dancing around the campfires at night.

We had days of warm sunshine and days of rain. Sometimes storms would rage for a whole day, filling the sky with rolling thunder and turning the little gullies at the foot of hills into fast-flowing streams.

One evening after the rain had finally stopped, the darkness around us was filled with dancing, flickering sparks of light.

"What is it?" Louvina asked, looking scared.

"Fireflies," answered Father.

Never in my life had I seen so many. They winked at me invitingly, on Father's shoulder, in Mother's hair, dotting the wagon cover, twinkling in the trees, everywhere.

One blinked right in front of me. I cupped my hand, then quickly closed it, but its light had already gone out.

"I'm going to catch one!" I said, jumping to my feet.

Louvina leapt up too. We raced in circles around and around the campfire, reaching and grabbing, but catching only air.

I felt the tiniest tickle in my palm.

"I've got one!" I cried.

"So have I!"

We crouched down next to the fire. Slowly and carefully, so as not to let our tiny captives escape, we opened our fists.

"Where is it?" Louvina whispered, puzzled.

But nothing was there.

Cynthia had been watching us, clapping her hands.

"Me do it!" she exclaimed. Then she too was running around on her short unsteady legs, her hands snatching at the sky, looking like a small ghost in her pale-yellow dress.

Music started up somewhere, the gay high jig of a fiddle. While Father and Mother watched, smiling from the shadows, the three of us twirled and danced until I was so dizzy I couldn't tell a firefly from the winking stars in the sky.

The next morning dawned bright and clear. Our wagon train was making good time when, early in the afternoon, we came to a small river called the Wakarusa. All the rains of the past few days had caused the river to rise, and the banks were so muddy that our wagons could not cross.

This was the first real obstacle we had come up against since leaving Independence. The captain called a halt and consulted with his council.

"It looks as if we will have to build a corduroy bridge," I heard Mr. Grant tell Father.

"That will not be so easy," Father replied. "There is not much wood hereabouts."

"We can do it," said Mr. Grant with his usual smiling confidence.

We camped beside the Wakarusa for several days.

Mother and Mrs. Grant brought out their washtubs and sat side by side in the grass, soaping and scrubbing, then hanging the wet clothes on lines strung from one wagon to the other. Afterward, while shirts and breeches, sheets and pillowcases and white underthings fluttered in the breeze, they turned their attention to making bread.

Louvina and I waded and splashed with Charlie and Matilda in the shallow water, and made mud pies with Cynthia. In the meantime John and David Grant, who had become his quiet shadow, went off with some of the men to scour the river bottoms for wood. They dragged back anything they could find: poles, small branches, brush. John was grinning with pride when he carried in a whole small tree.

The rest of the men, including Father, went to work. They chose the longest and strongest logs and laid them across from one bank of the river to the other. Then, crosswise on top of them, they began lining up the smaller poles and branches. While bumpy to ride across, this bridge would keep the wagons from miring down in the mud of the riverbanks.

As our men were working, I noticed that another wagon train had made camp a short distance above us on the river. They could see the bridge-building going on, I was sure. Yet none of their men came to lend a hand.

"Don't they want to cross too?" I asked Father. "Why aren't they helping out?"

Father just shook his head. "You will meet all kinds of people before this journey is over," he said soberly.

At last, after many days of hard work, the bridge was completed. We were ready to try the crossing.

Everyone was up early that morning. After breakfast

Mother was straightening out the bedding in the wagon while Father hitched up the oxen. It was his turn that day to lead the wagon train. I had just about finished my dish washing when I heard someone call, "Mister Todd! Mister Todd! Looky over there!"

We all looked. That other wagon train was coming around the bend of the river, heading straight for our bridge. Instantly I knew what they were planning to do. They were going to try to cross first. If they succeeded, all of their heavy wagons would ruin it for us.

Father did not hesitate.

"Quick!" he shouted. "Into the wagons!"

Mr. Grant ran back to warn the others. "Get ready to move out!" he bellowed at the top of his voice. "Hurry!"

"Hurry! Move out!" went up the cry from one wagon to another.

Everyone raced for their wagons. I stowed the last of the tin dishes in their box, handed Cynthia up to Mother, and scrambled into the wagon myself. Father stood next to the oxen, cracking his whip and shouting at Buck and Ben. The captain and several other men on horseback came riding up, urging them on. The oxen surged forward. In a moment they were going at a gallop.

I had never seen them move so fast. Father was hanging on to Buck's horn and running for dear life. John, mounted on Polly, was right beside him. Mother was half standing, holding tight to Cynthia, while behind her Louvina and I clung fast to the spring seat.

Leaning out, I strained to catch sight of the other train and promptly bumped my nose on the bouncing wagon bow. Their wagons were also racing for the bridge. Dogs barked, men and boys shouted, and whips popped. The rumble of so many heavy wagons sounded like thunder.

I held my breath. Could we possibly beat them? I wondered. It looked doubtful. But we must!

If we could just get our team started on the bridge first, we would be the winners. We were almost there, but so was the other wagon train. More whips cracked. Blows rained down on the backs of our poor oxen. Father shouted again, and they seemed to leap forward.

But just as our team was about to step onto the bridge, a horseman from the other train sprang in front of them. He sat there on his big chestnut-colored horse, red-faced and grinning, blocking the way.

We had lost.

Then something happened that I could hardly believe. Without a moment's hesitation Father raised his great whip and brought it down hard on horse and rider.

I stared in amazement. This was my gentle, patient father, who did not believe in violence, who could not be goaded into a fight, who never even raised his voice to correct a child. I hardly recognized him. In his face was a steely anger that I had never seen before.

Under his lash the red-faced horseman gave way. He wheeled and galloped off.

We had won!

"Hurrah for our train!" cried John in his thin shrill voice, throwing his hat in the air.

And in the wagons behind us everyone began to shout and cheer.

The other wagon train could do nothing but wait and watch while our long train crossed the river. It took half a day, as some of the poles and branches came loose and had to be repaired, and a few of the wagons bogged down

in the mud. As each one crossed, some of our young men
would wave back at the other train.

"Good-bye, Susanna!" they called mockingly. "Don't
you cry for me!"

We rested in the shade of a clump of cottonwood trees,
tired, our clothes and wagon cover splattered with mud,
but happy. Father was himself again. That stranger who
had risen up like an angry giant with his whip was gone.
The scene at the other side of the bridge seemed almost
like a dream to me, yet I knew it hadn't been a dream. I
kept stealing little glances at him, wondering.

A disapproving frown creased his forehead now as he
watched our boys taunting the other train.

"It's not very nice to rub their noses in it," he observed
in his familiar mild way.

But Mother smiled. "I think it serves them just right,"
she said.

Six

We had been traveling for six weeks now. Surely, I thought, we must be almost to Oregon. As the wagon train rolled along, I kept expecting to see that beautiful land that Father had told us about just beyond the next rise. But beyond the next rise would only be more waves of grass.

"We have come four hundred miles," Father told me when I asked him. "But we still have nearly two thousand miles ahead of us."

I stopped looking for Oregon on the horizon.

Soon after we crossed the Wakarusa, it began to rain again. For three days and nights the rain came pouring down, as if sloshing from a great tipped pan in the sky, making it impossible for our wagon train to move. While the men took care of the stock, did the milking, gathered wood, and tried to keep the fires going, most of the women and children stayed inside the wagons and tents. Everything was damp and covered with mud, and smoke from the fires was always in our eyes.

Louvina and I kept busy with our books. She was just beginning to read small words, and I was trying to memorize one of my favorite Longfellow poems. We taught Cynthia to count up to six, and to recite "Twinkle, Twinkle, Little Star."

One day Mother was not feeling very well. She seemed tired, and after lunch went to lie down in the wagon. Louvina and I were watching Cynthia inside the tent. But after a while we all grew tired of playing games and singing songs, and Cynthia began to get cranky.

"What is all this noise?"

John poked his head inside the tent door.

"Hi thar, Don!" Cynthia's pout suddenly turned into a smile.

"Hi thar, Cynthia!" He grinned back. Raindrops rolled off his rubber coat and hat, making a growing puddle on the tent floor. "How would you girls like it if I made some popcorn?"

"In the rain?" asked Louvina, her eyes wide.

"Why not? I couldn't get much wetter."

"I'll help you," I offered.

While Louvina and Cynthia watched from the tent door, John and I built up the campfire as hot as we could. Then we heated up the Dutch oven, and dropped in some popping corn.

As we crouched close to the fire, waiting for the sound of popping, the rain began coming down even harder. Smoke swirled into my eyes, making them stream with tears. I moved to the other side of the fire, but the smoke seemed to be following me. I couldn't see, nor could I hear any popping.

"Do you think the corn is ready?" I called to John over the wind and pounding rain.

"It must be," he answered.

By this time I hardly cared. I just wanted to get back inside the dry tent. John lifted the Dutch oven out of the fire and followed me inside.

"They're all burned!" Louvina cried in disappointment as he took off the lid.

About half of the kernels were black around the edges, and the other half hadn't popped.

John picked out a piece that wasn't so burned.

"It's good," he pronounced, chewing. "Try it."

So we all did. It was certainly not like the perfect puffy white popcorn that Mother used to make at home. But flavored with woodsmoke from the fire and eaten inside our warm tent with the rain beating down overhead, it tasted delicious to me.

"More!" demanded Cynthia.

And burned or not, we finished off all of that popcorn.

The fiddler in the nearby wagon kept playing his cheerful tunes in the evenings, and the old grandmother with the pipe kept calling to me, "You do be a fine little gal." Though Mother said her mind must be weak, I liked hearing it just the same. However, the wet, gloomy weather was beginning to take its toll on some of the families in camp. As I went to the stream for water or to collect sticks for the fire, I could hear men grumbling and women scolding. A few days earlier we had encountered a group of returning travelers. They were full of discouraging stories about the dangers and hardships that lay ahead. Listening to them, some people had become disheartened and talked of going back home.

When the sun finally came out again, most were ready to continue. But four families, including that of the very sick girl, Lucinda, turned back. I sat up on the spring seat watching their wagons grow smaller and smaller until they were only bright specks in the distance. And I wondered how they would do at the corduroy bridge.

It was a raw, chilly evening when we halted on the banks of the Kaw River. All of the recent rains and the melting snows of winter had swollen this small stream into a wide and mighty river. Looking at its muddy, swift-running currents, I couldn't help feeling a little shiver of fear. How were we ever going to cross all that water?

"We will have to wait a few days for the river to subside," Father told us, after returning from a meeting with the captain and the other men.

So once again we settled in to wait. We were not the only ones. All up and down the banks of the Kaw, other wagon trains were doing the same. Everywhere I looked, I saw rows of white wagon covers and tents, teams of horses and mules, huge herds of grazing cattle, barking dogs and running children.

We soon found out that there was a great deal of discouragement among the people camped there. By now many were weary of the journey and frightened of the stories they had heard. Every day more wagons were turning around and heading back home. Their fears spread to our wagon train. At night, worried voices talked around the campfires.

"What about this river crossing?" I heard a man from Ohio asking anxiously one evening. "I hear tell two men were drowned, along with a dozen cattle, a few days back."

"And folks are talking about seeing Indian war parties, all painted up, not far from here." That was Charlie and Matilda's father talking, a short man with bright-red hair just like Charlie's.

At that his wife began to cry. "Take me home, Jake," she pleaded. "Oh, I never did want to leave our family back in Pennsylvania."

It was no wonder people were beginning to waver. There were more discussions, a few heated arguments, and many tears. Once or twice I even thought I saw Father and Mother exchanging worried looks. Just for a moment I let myself imagine what it would be like to return home, driving by the familiar farms, with the new crops coming up fresh and green. Seeing all the folks we used to know look up, surprised to see us, then smile and wave. Passing by the schoolhouse, the meetinghouse. And then driving up to the gate at Grandma's house. At the sound of the wagon she would put down her sewing and look out the window, unable at first to believe her eyes. Then she would come running to meet us, the tears streaming down her face now tears of joy. And I would feel her warm arms around me again.

I looked at Father. Something in his face had changed, I thought, in the weeks since we had left Arkansas—and especially since crossing the bridge over the Wakarusa. The line of his jaw was sharper, firmer. And a determined light burned in those steady blue-gray eyes. Seeing it, I knew that he would not turn back.

Out of the hundred wagons that had set out from Independence, all but four turned around at the Kaw River. The four included the Grants and ourselves. Then there was a family named Tedrose, consisting of a couple with a baby and the young wife's unmarried brother. And finally another family with four children, the oldest of whom, Sarah Jane, was just a few months younger than I.

Sadly, Louvina and I watched as each of the returning

wagons got ready to pull out. The men hitched up their oxen in a dejected kind of way, it seemed to me. Yet some of the women were smiling. Our friends Charlie and Matilda were among the first to leave. They waved to us from the back of their wagon, their two bright heads framed above a crate of clucking chickens. The captain looked like just another tired farmer without his silver trumpet in his hand. The man who owned Towser turned back, as did the old gentleman who played the fiddle and the grandmother with the pipe. She leaned out of her wagon as it rolled by, and for the last time, I heard her say, "You do be a fine little gal."

Odd as she was, I was going to miss her. I lifted my hand and waved.

After being part of such a large train, it seemed strange and lonesome to be on our own again, without a captain to lead us. But we didn't have long to think about it. Preparations were underway for crossing the river. Some families from other wagon trains had gone to an old ferryboat downstream, but those who ran it charged high prices, and it was not considered very safe. So, after discussions among the men, our four families decided to wait for the river to go down and then cross on our own. To do this the wagon beds had to be turned into boats.

I watched as all of the contents of each wagon were unpacked and piled up on the ground. The wagon beds were taken off the running gear and turned upside down. Then the men went to work, caulking each seam with resin and tar, inside and out, so no water would be able to seep in. The job was messy and took hours to complete. After that the wagon beds were dragged down to the water's edge.

Day by day the river had been slowly going down. Now at last it was low enough for us to try to cross. The wagon beds were in the water, loaded up and tied to the bank. But first the animals had to be driven across. Father and Mr. Grant, mounted on our two horses, rounded up all the stock and headed them for the riverbank.

"Ho-ay! Ho-ay!" they shouted, cracking their whips.

Cattle and loose horses milled around at the water's edge. The fearful animals did not seem to want to take the plunge. Some turned around, trying to run away, but the stinging whips forced them forward.

"Ho-ay!"

Now they were in shallow water. I saw Bright, one of our oxen, stumble, and the others appeared to walk right over him. Then all at once they were swimming.

As the animals reached deeper water, most of the cattle settled down to steady swimming. But the loose horses plunged and snorted and kept trying to turn back. Father and Mr. Grant had to keep their own horses constantly moving and their whips flying.

Just as they were nearing the opposite bank, I noticed that Daisy, our little two-year-old heifer, was in trouble. She was struggling frantically in the swift current. I could see her light-brown head rising and falling.

"Father!" I screamed. But he could not hear me above the rushing water. And he was too far away to reach her.

Then suddenly I saw Daisy turn over on her side and float away down the river.

"Oh!" cried John, standing next to me. "Our two-year-old yearling is drowning! What can we do?"

Louvina began to sob quietly. John kept waving his arms and shouting in his high-pitched voice, "Our two-

year-old yearling is drowning!" Something was wrong with what he was saying, I thought vaguely. A yearling couldn't be two years old. Nearby, Sarah Jane and her two younger brothers were beginning to smile. But I couldn't smile. Our favorite little heifer was gone.

All the rest of the animals made it safely across. In a few minutes Father and Mr. Grant came back to help with the wagons. Ours was to go first. A long, strong rope was attached to the front of the wagon bed. Mr. Tedrose, a tall, muscular young man with a blond mustache, took the end of it. He swam the river on his horse, then secured the rope around a good-sized tree on the opposite bank. Another rope was fastened in the same way behind. Father and John each picked up an oar.

"We are ready," said Father.

My knees were trembling uncontrollably as I stepped on board that floating wagon. All I could think about was Daisy and how she had looked in that moment when the rushing water took her away. Mother held Cynthia in her arms. Louvina, her cheeks still streaked with tears, clutched my hand as if she never would let it go. In a moment Father had pushed off and he and John were paddling.

All the work of caulking the wagon had been worthwhile. Hardly a drop leaked in. Slowly, with Father and John working hard at the oars, our lumbering craft moved out to the middle of the river. Now we were in that fast-moving current, very close to the spot where Daisy had been lost. White spray flew through the air. Beneath my feet I could feel the wagon bed being tossed and pulled. Fear moved up to my stomach, which began to churn like the swift water. I had to close my eyes.

When I opened them again, I was sure that we too were being swept away.

"Pull!" Father shouted to John. "Harder!"

I realized that now I was gripping Louvina's hand, so tight that tears were squeezing out of her eyes again.

John was paddling furiously. Father, on the downstream side, worked just as hard. On the opposite shore Mr. Tedrose was struggling to tighten the rope around the tree. The wagon creaked and groaned. It seemed as if the raging water might tear it apart.

Then, very slowly, we began to swing toward shore. Moments later I felt our wagon softly nudge against the riverbank. John jumped out and tied it fast, and Louvina and I hugged each other in relief.

As we stepped onto solid land once more, I looked back at the river. Where was Rover? When we started out I had seen him jump into the water behind us, then had lost track of him after I closed my eyes. I scanned the rough water for a glimpse of his white face, his curling black-tipped tail. But I couldn't see any sign of him. Had he, like Daisy, been washed away by that fierce current?

Then suddenly behind me, I heard a familiar flapping shake. And there he was, dripping wet and limping a little, but safe.

"Rover!" cried Louvina.

Wet as he was, we gathered him into our arms, and his tail beat joyfully against the muddy earth.

We stood on the riverbank, watching while the other wagons crossed one by one. It took several hours, but all of them made it safely. After that each family was busy setting up their wagons again, sorting out belongings and repacking them, drying out all of the clothing and bedding and sacks of food that had gotten damp in the crossing.

It was not until late that evening, when our family was gathered around the campfire, that I thought again of Daisy. I remembered the rough-soft feel of her tongue licking my fingers, making me want to laugh and squirm at the same time. I remembered the way she used to look at me with her moist dark-brown saucer eyes when she came to be petted.

My own eyes filled up with tears.

Father had been reading to us from the Bible. He stopped in the middle of a verse and looked across at me.

"It could have been much worse, you know, Mary Ellen," he said quietly. "We must be thankful that all of our people and their wagons and teams made it safely across."

Thinking about it, I knew he was right. What if it had been Buck or Ben who had been lost? Or Mr. Grant, or John, or—Father? A long shiver ran down my backbone at the unimaginable thought.

But tears ran down my cheeks anyway. I cried for my pet calf whom I would not see or touch ever again. And I was crying for other things too: our warm, wonderful barn and our house, and every little tree and piece of earth that I had known, and Grandma—everything back home that was lost to me now.

Because it was certain now that we were not going back. We had crossed the river and we had to go on.

Seven

We left behind the grassy prairies of Kansas and moved on to the plains of Nebraska. Here the grass was shorter, the soil more sandy. The occasional clumps of beautiful oak trees we had seen were replaced by sparsely scattered cottonwoods and willows on the banks of streams. And instead of the sweet sounds of the lark and the mockingbird, we heard only the lone hoot of an owl.

Looking over this vast flat barren land, the men seemed more keenly aware of the great distance still to be traveled to reach Oregon. They talked about it one evening as the sun was going down.

"We need to make more speed," urged Mr. Tedrose. An eager, adventurous young man, he always hated to see other wagons pass us by. "It is already almost the first of June."

Sarah Jane's father, a lean, sandy-haired man with ears like the handles on one of Father's pottery jugs, agreed. "With good weather, we ought to be able to make eighteen or twenty miles a day."

Mr. Grant nodded.

But Father's face was thoughtful. "We must be careful not to push the animals too hard," he cautioned. "We have to keep them in good condition if they are to take us all the way."

So our small wagon train pushed ahead. To make better speed we spent a little less time grazing the stock at noon and didn't stop at night until it was almost dark. The weather now was more favorable, although we still had occasional rain showers and cold, raw winds. Most days we were able to make fifteen or sixteen miles, according to the guidebook, and once Father said we had gone twenty miles.

Sarah Jane liked to walk too, and we soon became friends. Walking along next to our wagon, her straw-colored hair poking out from under her yellow-checked sunbonnet, she told me all about her home back in Kentucky.

"We lived in a real plantation house made of brick," she said, smiling at the memory, "with a great big front porch and flowers growing everywhere. The kitchen was a separate building out back. And I had a swing in a mulberry tree."

Out in the fields her father grew tobacco, corn, and pumpkins, muskmelons and watermelons, and the most wonderful sweet potatoes. But he had slaves to do all the work.

That explained it, I thought. The way her father never looked quite comfortable in his rough clothes, his slowness in yoking his oxen and loading up his wagon in the mornings.

"My mama has never washed clothes before," she told me, "or fixed a single meal. But she's doing right well at it, I think."

"Why did you want to leave your plantation to go out west?" I asked her, puzzled.

Sarah Jane's face turned suddenly grave. "It's on account of my baby sister, Luella," she explained. "We lived in low river country, and she kept getting the fever. The doctor told my daddy she wouldn't live to grow up unless we moved."

We found very little to look at as the oxen plodded slowly along in the dust. Once we passed an abandoned Indian village, now just a few tepee poles over which buffalo hides had been stretched. Now and then we would come upon a prairie-dog town. As far as we could see were piles of mounded earth, with holes in the center. The prairie dogs, who looked like fat brown squirrels, seemed to be keeping watch, sitting up on their hind legs next to their holes. When they saw us, they would bark furiously in little yipping voices, then tumble into their holes. They looked so funny that Sarah Jane and I burst out laughing.

Once in a while too we would pass fields dotted with flowers: wild bluebells, buttercups, purple and white lupine, and many others that I could not name. Louvina jumped down from the wagon, and the three of us gathered up armloads of flowers. We decorated our wagons with bouquets, and sometimes braided them into wreaths. One afternoon we placed a wreath on top of Cynthia's short yellow curls.

"I crown you Queen of the May," pronounced Louvina.

"Queen May!" repeated Cynthia, bouncing up and down and laughing delightedly.

For the rest of that day she wore the drooping circle of flowers like a lopsided crown. Even at bedtime, when

Mother tried to take it off, I could hear her protesting, "Queen May! Queen May!"

Herds of fleet-footed antelope and buffalo, with their dark hunched shoulders and shaggy manes, could sometimes be seen running in the distance. Mr. Grant, who loved to hunt, kept going out after them until he finally succeeded in shooting an antelope. He divided up the meat among the four families. It tasted good while it lasted—like veal, Mother said. But nothing lasted very long at our table anymore, except molasses, of which we had a whole keg. With every mile we traveled our appetites seemed to grow, and I was always hungry.

Fuel for the campfires was growing scarce, and so was good, clear drinking water. As I walked along, I picked up any little twigs I could find for firewood and poked them into the chairs hanging on the back of the wagon. Once I thought I saw, in the distance up ahead, a great shimmering lake surrounded by trees. But as we drew closer, it suddenly disappeared.

"Where did the lake go?" I asked Father.

"It was not real," he answered. "Your lake was just a mirage."

Sometimes my eyes ached from looking out over those bare treeless plains in the afternoon sun. But in the evening, when the round red ball of sun slowly sank in the west, washing land and sky with a rosy glow, it was beautiful.

One afternoon I was walking alone beside the wagon, my eyes on the ground, searching for twigs. The hot midday sun beat down on my head, making me feel drowsy. The wagon wheels slowly turned. The oxen picked up their feet and put them down. The white wagon top swayed against the bright-blue sky, while underneath the milk pail swung back and forth, back and forth. Even Father, sitting high on the spring seat, his shoulders bent, his big whip still, seemed almost asleep.

All at once I heard Rover up ahead start barking. I looked up. Galloping toward us across the flat dusty plain was a band of Indians.

It was the first time in our journey that I had seen Indians up close. As they came nearer, I could make out fifteen or twenty of them, sitting straight on spotted ponies. They were all painted in bright war paint, and some wore headdresses of white eagle feathers that fluttered in the breeze. They looked so strange and wild that my breath caught in my throat and my heart began bumping crazily inside my chest.

Dropping my twigs, I scrambled quickly into the back of the wagon. In my haste my foot kicked the milk pail, and it slopped over. I grabbed Louvina and drew her down so we both were hidden from sight, then pulled the bedclothes over our heads.

Now the wagons creaked to a stop. Ahead of us the Indians were talking to Mr. Grant, but I could not make out their words. Gradually my pounding heart slowed to its normal beat. Peeping out, I saw one of the Indians, who seemed to be their leader, making gestures with his hands. He was tall and coppery brown and sat as straight as a tree trunk. With his dark glittering eyes and beaked nose, he reminded me of some kind of fierce painted bird.

"Go fight Crows," he said in a deep, harsh voice.

Another Indian was pointing off into the distance.

"I think they are trying to tell us that they have no quarrel with the whites," said Father in a low voice.

Cynthia was awake now and starting to whimper.

"Hush!" whispered Mother, rocking her.

Up ahead there was more confusing talk and more signs. Then, abruptly, the Indians were gone.

I watched them gallop away until at last they became just far-off puffs of dust. But even as relief washed over me, I felt a little twinge of shame. If Grandma had been here, she would not have been afraid. She would not have spilled the milk and hidden herself away under the bedclothes. I knew Grandma. She would have drawn herself up and looked that big Indian right in the eye.

I was not the only one who had been frightened, however. That night an uneasy feeling hung over our camp. The men talked in low voices. The women wore worried looks as they prepared the evening meal. Cynthia fussed more than usual, clinging to Mother's skirts. And although I tried hard not to, I found myself looking over my shoulder at the slightest noise. The stories we had heard about Indians in war paint were true. Maybe those other stories about stealing horses and massacring white families were true too.

Father tried to calm our fears.

"All those terrible tales we have been hearing are exaggerated," he told Louvina and me. "Most Indians, like the Kaws we saw today, are peaceful toward the white people, and most wagon trains are not bothered by them. But the Indians do have reason to be unhappy. You know, all this country once belonged to them. For years the whites have been crowding them out. They have killed their buffalo and taken their land. They have not treated them with fairness."

Thinking about Indians in this way made me feel more

kindly toward them and less frightened. Still, in the black stillness of midnight, when I heard wolves howl and Rover answer with his low rumbling growl, I couldn't help remembering those stories and wondering if Indians were creeping up on our camp in the darkness.

Once in a while Sarah Jane and I were allowed to ride John and David Grant's horses. This made a nice change in the monotony of our days. Of course Mother insisted on my riding sidesaddle, with my long, full skirt down over my ankles.

"It is the only way for a young lady to ride," she said firmly.

I thought about how John sat his horse, his head low, his legs locked around Polly's sides as he urged her to a gallop, and I opened my mouth to protest. But Father was looking at me.

"Mary Ellen," he began, with a warning frown.

So I said nothing. Although inside I was simmering with resentment, I rode sidesaddle.

Sarah Jane and I were on horseback one day, driving the small herd of cattle at the back of the train. It was another slow, quiet, warm afternoon. We were talking about the differences in cows once you got to know them.

"Take those two." Sarah Jane pointed at two black-and-white ones. "They look about alike. But that one is lazy. And the other one is just plain ornery."

"That brown heifer of Mr. Grant's reminds me of Daisy," I told her. "Only she isn't as friendly. You should have seen how Daisy would butt her head at me when she wanted to be petted."

We rode along in silence for a few minutes.

"My favorite cow of ours was a big red one that my

daddy used to call Pink," Sarah Jane said. "Now, that cow had a mind of her own. My mama said she was opposed to going to Oregon. The very first morning after we left, she turned up missing. My daddy rode back a few miles, and don't you know he found her heading for home just as fast as she could go. Pink did that three or four times. Then one morning, somewhere in Illinois, we lost her. My daddy thinks someone stole her. But my mama is sure she is home by now. Pink always was a sensible cow, she says."

At that moment I looked up to see five Indians riding right next to us.

They were not in war paint. Their chests were bare, and their black hair was cut close to their scalps, except for something like a rooster comb on top, colored red. They sat stiff and solemn on their ponies, not trying to speak to us.

What could they want?

Again, my heart started thumping madly. I looked over at Sarah Jane. Underneath her faded yellow sunbonnet her eyes were dark and very large. I knew she was as scared as I was. We were a fair distance behind the wagons, and no one else seemed to have seen the Indians.

They kept riding along right next to us. One of their ponies was so close that I could plainly see its round, red-brown side, its rider's leather leggings and brightly beaded moccasins. I didn't dare look up into that Indian's face. But for a brief moment I found myself marveling at how he could ride without a saddle or bridle.

Now the Indians were talking among themselves. They made low guttural sounds, gesturing. They seemed to be taking particular notice of the cattle we were driving.

Maybe they meant to steal them.

I need Father, I thought. Now. I stared at the back of our wagon. If only he would look over his shoulder and see what was happening. Again my eyes met Sarah Jane's. And almost as if by unspoken agreement, we both urged our horses toward the wagon.

Just then Father turned around and saw the Indians.

"Whoa!" he shouted to the oxen.

Seeing him, the Indians halted too. For a long moment they seemed to hesitate, looking at each other. Then, laughing, they kicked their ponies and galloped away.

My knees were shaking so hard I could barely stand as Sarah Jane and I slid down from the horses' backs. Without a backward look she ran off toward her wagon. Father jumped down from the spring seat and gathered me into his arms. I felt like a trembling rabbit returned to its nest.

"It's all right, honey," he murmured against my hair. "They are gone now. Everything is all right."

Mother smiled down at me from the wagon.

"Don't cry, Mary Ellen," she said. "You were very brave."

Louvina was looking at me as if I had performed some heroic deed. Father's arms were strong around me. But though he kept comforting me, and Mother kept telling me how brave I had been, my knees refused to stop shaking.

For days after that Sarah Jane and I made sure we walked close to the wagons.

Eight

"Be not like dumb, driven cattle," I proclaimed, my arms stretched out, one finger pointing upward, the way I'd seen our young minister do during his sermons back home in Arkansas. "Be a hero in the strife!"

"Mary Ellen!"

I turned, startled, to find Louvina frowning at me.

"I don't think it is very nice to talk about our poor cattle that way," she admonished me.

I had thought I was alone, washing the noontime dishes in a tiny trickle of a stream, with only the cattle for company. They grazed quietly nearby, a ragged patchwork of brown and white and black, their heads down, tails switching at flies.

"I was just practicing my Longfellow poem," I explained, bending down to rinse the last two tin plates.

"Oh." Magically, her frown changed to her usual sunny smile. "Well, that's all right then," she said. And she skipped away.

But after that, whenever I recited this verse, I felt as if I ought to apologize to our cattle, who were so patiently pulling our wagon along. They never complained or shirked their work. When Father lifted the yoke and said, "Come, Buck and Ben," the two lead oxen always put their heads obediently under it. Dumb and driven they might be, but they seemed like heroes to me.

Our fast pace of the last two weeks was beginning to take its toll on all of our animals. Some of the oxen had sore shoulders, where their neck bows rubbed against the flesh. Father and John cleansed the sores, rubbed the wood of the neck bows smooth, and sometimes padded them. Their feet were also starting to become tender. Our cow Lillie had almost stopped giving milk, so we couldn't have one of our favorite evening meals, mush and milk. And Rover didn't chase squirrels anymore or play, but just walked with a little limp behind the wagon.

On the day of our longest march I saw him lagging farther and farther behind. Finally he gave up and lay down in the dust.

"Father! Wait!" I cried.

Father stopped the team, and I ran back. Rover lay with his head between his paws, his sad brown eyes looking up at me, his tail thumping against the ground.

"Come, Rover," I coaxed, trying to lift him up. But the poor dog could not stand.

"It is his feet," said Father, when John and I carried him to the wagon. "They are all cut and sore."

Although Mother did not approve of having a dog in the wagon, she let him stay just this once. As we rode along, she stitched up some canvas shoes for him. That night Louvina and I bathed Rover's feet and put on healing powders. The next morning, after breakfast, we dressed him in his little shoes.

At first he tried to chew them off. Finally, though, he decided to endure them. It was so strange to see a dog wearing shoes that we all had a good laugh. And Rover hung his head as if he were ashamed.

Mother too seemed more and more tired. Some evenings she did not feel up to preparing supper and just sat in her chair, directing us about the cooking. Those nights all we had to eat was bacon and frying-pan bread. And, of course, our everlasting molasses.

Still, the men kept pressing forward. One day we again made close to twenty miles, descending from the high plains through a line of low, barren hills, like drifts of sand thrown up by the wind, and into the wide valley of the Platte River. In front of us lay the river: a mile across, it seemed to me, swift and swollen and muddy yellow in color. Its fast-flowing water was dotted with islands, and on them grew green bushes and trees. But no trees at all, not even a slip of willow or cottonwood, could be seen on the low riverbanks. The land was so flat, the sky so high, and the river so wide that all I could do was stand and stare. Never, I thought, had I seen a world so large.

Looking at it in the gray dusk, the Platte seemed impossible to cross. But the next morning, when Father measured the water with a pole, we were amazed to find that it was only about three feet deep.

So the wagon beds were raised several inches with blocks, to make sure no water would run in. And ropes were attached to the front, so the men riding ahead on horseback could help out if necessary. Mr. Tedrose went first, looking for the best route to cross, as we had heard about the dangers of quicksand.

Then whips snapped and cattle bawled.

"Up there, Buck and Ben!" shouted Father.

Reluctantly the teams started into the river.

It was a long and slow crossing. As the water crept higher and higher up the wagon bed, I remembered the crossing of the Kaw. I began to feel dizzy and closed my eyes. But our wagon made it to the other side without even a sack of flour or any of the bedding getting wet. The others did almost as well. The only loss in the crossing was David Grant's hat, which flew off and quickly sank in the muddy water.

At a place called Grand Island our trail joined with another one. Here the road had been so deeply cut by passing wagons that sometimes the sand came all the way up to the wheel hubs.

Suddenly we were once again in daily contact with other wagon trains. This trail, we were told, came from Council Bluffs, Iowa. One day a friendly family gave us a newspaper. It was rare that Father would take time to rest before dinner. But that afternoon he sat down, his back leaning against the wagon tongue, and eagerly devoured every page of that folded and torn month-old newspaper.

"It seems that the Southern problem is waxing warm," he told Mother at supper. "The talk everywhere is of slavery. And Abraham Lincoln is attracting attention with his speeches." Mr. Lincoln, a young lawyer, had married Father's first cousin in Illinois.

The next day I overheard Father discussing the subject with the other men. It was late in the afternoon after we had made camp. The men had put the animals out to feed. Coming back, they had to search a large area to find enough fuel for the campfires. While the evening meal was being prepared, each of them was doing various chores: greasing wagon wheels, soaking a wheel so that the wood would not dry out and the iron tire fall off, tightening up brake blocks, splicing whip lashes.

"You know," said Sarah Jane's father, "we are doing niggers' work."

I was shocked to hear him use that word. Father would never permit us to speak that way.

"All honest work is honorable," Father replied quietly.

Sarah Jane's father shook his head, pulling on his short chin whiskers. "Those people are only fit to be bossed and do dirty work," he said.

Mr. Grant bounced up from where he had been bent over a wheel. "We live in a free country," he burst out, his face turning red as it did whenever he was agitated. "No man, either white or black, should be a slave for another."

"You do not know them as I do," Sarah Jane's father insisted, "or you wouldn't speak that way."

Just at that moment Mother called me to fetch water from the river.

Sarah Jane and I walked along side by side, swinging our buckets.

"You know," she said after a moment, "my father has had slaves and he knows what he is talking about."

"But my father reads his Bible and he knows what is right," I answered.

We were both silent as we dipped our pails into the river.

"Anyway," Sarah Jane added as we started back, "you can't trust one of them."

"You can't trust some white people!" I retorted. "I think the Negroes should be freed."

Bright spots of pink burned on her cheeks. "Never!" she cried.

We walked the rest of the way back to camp in silence.

But in the days that followed there was little time for political discussions. A much more pressing problem was on the minds of the men. It was the condition of our animals. Father was worried about how thin the cattle and horses were becoming. He thought we should slow down to give them more time to graze and rest. Mr. Grant agreed with him, but the other men did not.

Mr. Tedrose dismissed the idea with an impatient wave of his hand.

"At that rate we'll never get through to Oregon," he said. "Other trains are passing us every day now. They will be the ones who get the best land, and we will have to take what is left. My animals are sound. They will not wear out."

"We are already two weeks behind schedule," added Sarah Jane's father. "We cannot afford to lose any more time."

I could hear their raised voices talking long after I went to bed. At breakfast the next morning Father's face was somber.

"It looks as if we are going to have to go our separate ways," he told us.

That noon, when we stopped to have our lunch and let the cattle graze for an hour, Sarah Jane's family and the Tedroses went on without us.

It was sad to have to say good-bye to Sarah Jane. I thought about all the miles we had walked together and the good times we'd had. Telling stories, laughing at the antics of the prairie dogs, picking flowers, herding the cattle together on horseback. And that bad time with the Indians. Would we ever meet again? I wondered.

"Good-bye!" I called, waving my arms, as her wagon rolled slowly away. "Good luck!"

"Good luck to you!" she shouted back.

We kept waving to each other as her wagon, with Sarah Jane's yellow sunbonnet beside it, grew smaller and smaller in the distance. Finally it disappeared in the shimmering sun.

That afternoon I walked by myself along the warm sandy road. Dust filled my throat. The sand reflected the heat of the sun back into my face, making perspiration trickle down my cheeks. Looking around, I could see nothing to break the monotony: not a stick or a stone, a bird or a flower. I began to wonder about Father. Were he and Mr. Grant being sensible, or was it possible that they were too careful? If others could travel fast, why couldn't we?

As Father was stacking the wood for the campfire that evening, I asked him about it.

"Mary Ellen," he said in his calm, reasonable voice, looking straight at me, "there is an old saying: 'The more haste, the less speed.' Surely you must have noticed the skeletons we have passed of oxen that had to be abandoned along the way. It is essential that we take care of our animals. Otherwise they will not be able to carry us safely through."

I understood what he was saying. From time to time I

had seen the bones of dead oxen bleached white by the sun. Still, it seemed terrible to have our friends go on without us, leaving us alone.

That night, as darkness closed in and the voices of coyotes and wolves rang out across the empty plains, I felt more lonesome than ever before. I huddled close to my sleeping sister, trying to get warm. For comfort my thoughts turned back to the little house we had left behind in Arkansas. I tried to imagine my bed tucked up under the roof. Mother's white curtains puffed out in a breeze. The easy chairs in front of the big stone fireplace, with a fire burning snug and warm. Father's pottery wheel out in the shed, turning out a plump jug, a tall, graceful pitcher. But somehow or other I couldn't quite bring them into focus.

How could I forget in just a few short weeks?

Then, wrapping her starry quilt close around me like a cocoon, I thought of Grandma. More than ever now I needed to remember her smiling face. But suddenly even Grandma's face was lost to me. It seemed to hover somewhere just out of reach.

Shivering, I waited for morning to come again.

Nine

It was mid-June now, the month of roses. I looked for
wild rose bushes as I walked behind the wagon on the
heavy, hot sand road that wound next to the Platte River.
And finally one day I found one, its tight pale-pink buds
almost ready to burst into bloom.

As we made our way up the river, we passed by Fort
Kearney, a small military post with buildings made of
sun-dried bricks. These were the first man-made struc-
tures we had seen in over two hundred miles. We were
hoping to reach the next fort, Fort Laramie in Wyoming,
by the Fourth of July. That would be close to seven
hundred miles we had traveled since leaving Independence. But even then, Father said, we still would not be
halfway to Oregon.

With all of his care some of the oxen were still limping.
And Rover kept on lagging far behind the wagon.

"Here, Rover!" called John one day, flashing his quick
grin. "I'll give you a lift."

Leaning over, he scooped up Rover and placed him in front of him on his horse.

"Ride horsie!" Cynthia laughed and clapped her pudgy hands.

But Rover wasn't happy with the idea, and neither was Polly. She kicked and Rover struggled so desperately that finally John had to put him down.

"All right, have it your way," he said.

The next day he tried again. And again. And after a few days both dog and horse became resigned to it. It was a comical sight to see Rover sitting up straight in the saddle in front of John, barking at rabbits and prairie dogs as he rode along.

We continued to meet many other wagon trains. One which I especially noticed had the words "Sure and Swift" painted on its wagon covers. The wagons in this train were pulled by fast mules instead of oxen, and its people dressed in style. They seemed to be looking down their noses at us as they sailed past our slow-moving wagons. Mrs. Grant said she had heard that they had music in their camp every night, and used silverware and real white table linens for dinner. After this train passed us, they would camp for several days so we would catch up with them. But then a day or two later, their mules would go breezing by us again. I couldn't help feeling a little twinge of envy at how easy their journey seemed to be.

The road we traveled on now had been beaten down by thousands of hooves. On dry days billows of dust rose from beneath our wheels. And when it rained, tiny streams turned into bogs, and mosquitoes swarmed, making a small cloud around each of the oxen's heads.

David Grant called them "gallinippers." We slapped

and scratched. Poor Cynthia's face was covered with huge red welts. Some nights we could hardly sleep because of all the gallinippers buzzing in our ears.

We were also having trouble with drinking water. The water in the Platte was so warm and muddy, it was barely fit to drink. We had to let it settle before using it. One time John measured the water in his tin cup and found that the bottom fourth was all mud.

Since we had crossed the Platte, wood for the fires had been getting scarcer and scarcer. One evening there was none to be found anywhere.

"We can't cook without fires," said Mrs. Grant in dismay. "And how can we have fires without wood?"

Mr. Grant looked at her, a hint of a held-in grin showing in his eyes.

"I'll show you," he offered.

In just a few minutes he had picked up an armful of buffalo chips, the dried old droppings from passing buffalo that littered the grass around us. Setting a match to them, he soon had a good hot fire.

But both Mrs. Grant and Mother turned away, covering their noses at the smell.

"I can't cook our food over a fire like that," Mother complained to Father. Her face was pale, as if she might actually be sick.

"It is hard, Angelina, I know," he replied gently. "But we have no choice. If there is nothing to cook with except buffalo chips, we must use them and be grateful for them."

Mother still did not like it. However, buffalo chips were the only fuel available. At first she handled them gingerly, wearing gloves and holding them out at arm's length with a look of great distaste. But within a few days she had

Louvina and me helping her, piling them into our aprons with hardly a thought.

As we moved along, we began to see more and more signs of distress ahead. Sometimes it was worn-out oxen abandoned to the wolves. Sometimes it was broken-down wagons with tires off and wheel spokes snapped. In some cases, Father told us, what was left had been converted into a two-wheeled cart so that the travelers could go on. Another time we came upon the remains of an ox that looked just like Star, one of Mr. Tedrose's oxen. I thought of Sarah Jane, and wondered how she was making out. And quite frequently now we would see a freshly dug grave where some poor traveler had been buried.

One afternoon, as I was walking along, keeping an eye out for more roses, I saw a wagon moving toward us at an unusually fast pace. As it came closer, I could make out a bearded man with wild-looking eyes, beating his oxen with a whip to make them go faster. His wife and about six fair-haired, freckle-faced children peered out at us from inside the wagon, their faces full of fear.

"It is the cholera!" the man called to us without stopping his wagon. "It is terrible upriver. Whole families are being wiped out. So we are just going back home!"

And snapping his whip again, he moved hastily on his way.

Mother's mouth tightened at this news, and I thought I could see new lines of worry creasing Father's forehead. We had already heard rumors of an epidemic of this dreaded disease raging along the river. It struck suddenly, with severe vomiting, diarrhea, and high fever. Its victims would lapse into unconsciousness and often be dead within hours.

That night Father and Mother and the Grants talked for a long time in low, concerned voices. But there was nothing to do, they decided, but go on, taking as many precautions as possible. We planned to keep moving as fast as we could. And, Mother told Louvina and Cynthia and me, we were to stay close to the wagon at all times.

Soon we began passing other wagons that had been forced to halt because of illness. Father and Mother tried to help some of these families by offering our medicines and the small supply of milk that Blackie still gave. Father also gave advice on caring for the sick. Others, in their frantic haste to escape the place of infection, kept on traveling as fast as they could, their sick ones jouncing and jolting inside the wagons. And every day we passed more fresh graves.

One day, just after we had stopped for nooning, Louvina came to Mother, her usually pink cheeks suddenly pale beneath her sunbonnet.

"I don't feel well," she complained in a small voice.

In just a few minutes she was violently sick.

"We will have to make camp right here," Father decided quickly.

He and John set up the tent some distance from the wagon, made up a bed inside, and carried Louvina to it.

"Now everyone must stay far away," he warned.

Only an hour later Cynthia also turned pale and began to whimper and hold on to her stomach. Soon she was just as sick as Louvina. Father laid her down next to Louvina inside the tent.

For the remainder of the day he took charge of caring for them. The rest of us hurried about, trying to help. John and I had to look after the animals, keep a fire continuously burning, fetch water and keep it hot, and help Mother with the cooking. Louvina and Cynthia were suffering from terrible cramps and chills, and they were constantly in need of something. As I went from one chore to another, all I could think about was that the thing we had dreaded most had happened. My two little sisters had cholera.

The Grants made camp a considerable distance away, to keep clear of the infection. But they promised to wait for us, offering to do anything they could to help. There was not much to be done, though, without a doctor or other medical help nearby.

That night Father slept just outside the door of the tent. John was underneath the wagon, and Mother and I were alone inside it. It was close to midnight when she came to bed. I couldn't sleep and was trying to read by the light of our little oil lamp hung up on the ridge pole. But I couldn't seem to read either.

Mother's face looked different than I had ever seen it as she slowly removed the combs from her hair. It tumbled down over her shoulders, soft and shining, as yellow almost as Cynthia's in the lamplight. The light illuminated the planes of her cheekbones and the curve of her neck. She seemed beautiful to me in that moment. But then I saw her eyes. In them was a strange awful blankness, as if she had been stunned by a blow she had not seen coming. The dim light made it hard to be sure, but I thought I saw tears streaking her cheeks.

"Have you said your prayers, Mary Ellen?" she asked in a voice that was barely a whisper.

Without waiting for me to reply, she knelt down.

Quietly there in the shadowy dark I joined her. And side by side we offered up our prayers for my sisters.

" . . . Bless them and keep them, oh Lord," Mother finished, her voice breaking a little just at the end. "Amen."

I felt tears beginning to burn in my eyes.

"Amen," I echoed.

Outside the night seemed suddenly hushed. Maybe, I thought hopefully, they were sleeping.

Then in the darkness I felt Mother's fingers reach out and touch mine. Cool and firm, they squeezed once and were gone. But their touch lingered on like a prayer.

"Try to sleep," she said softly a minute later, blowing out the lamp.

And surprisingly I did.

When I awoke the next morning, I was puzzled for a moment to find myself alone in the wagon. Then, with a pang, I remembered Louvina and Cynthia.

"How are they?" I asked anxiously, poking my head outside.

In the daylight, her hair tucked back tidily, wearing her apron, Mother looked herself again, piling coals on top of the Dutch oven to cook the biscuits. Only her eyes were grave.

"Your father says that Cynthia is not nearly as bad as Louvina," she answered. "But Louvina is very sick."

I felt as if I ought to whisper as I moved about that morning, doing my chores. On my way down to the river for water I passed by the tent. Through the opening I caught a glimpse of Louvina's face. It was so white and still, I hardly recognized it as my sister. Feeling a sharp pinch of fear way down in my insides, I hurried past.

Many other wagons were stopped near us. The cholera epidemic had been growing worse by the day, and nearly every evening we heard about a new illness or death.

Sometimes it was the father or mother or an elderly relative, but most often it seemed to be the children. One night seventeen new graves were dug near the river.

While we were suffering with our fear and anxiety, the animals made the most of their unexpected rest. Rover lay sleeping in the sun for hours. The horses rolled around in the grass, then fed to their hearts' content. The cattle would graze until they had their fill, lie down and chew their cuds, then lazily get to their feet and start grazing once more.

Meanwhile Father kept his lonely vigil beside Louvina and Cynthia, hour after hour, day after day. He would not allow the rest of us anywhere near them, for fear of our catching the infection. Every little while Mother would take food to him, asking quietly, "How is Louvina?" But Father just shook his head, his eyes filled with despair.

In a few days Cynthia was well enough to be taken out of the tent. Before she could be allowed near us, though, she had to be bathed and all of her clothing and bedding disinfected. Father piled it all in the washtub and poured boiling water over it, then hung everything out in the sun to dry. We made up a comfortable bed for her on the spring seat, and Father carried her to it.

I was so happy to see her again. But she was weak and fretful, and needed constant care. John and I tried for three days before we could make her smile.

One morning I heard Father asking Mother for our small looking glass. He took it into the tent. A few minutes later he handed it back to her.

"What is the matter?" I asked.

Mother's breath seemed to catch as she answered. "He couldn't tell if Louvina was breathing or not. So he held the looking glass over her mouth to see if any moisture collected on it."

I felt something squeezing my stomach.

"And did it?" I forced myself to ask in a whisper.

"He thinks so. But we cannot know yet how it will turn out. We can only wait and pray."

For two days Louvina hovered between life and death. Father looked so exhausted that Mother begged him to rest, but he rarely did. At times he was sure she was dead, she lay so very still.

Once I heard him repeating the Twenty-third Psalm. ". . . Yea, though I walk through the valley of the shadow of death . . ."

His voice cracked, and he could not go on.

So I finished for him. " . . . I will fear no evil. For thou art with me; thy rod and thy staff they comfort me."

Sometimes I wondered if it could be my fault that this had happened to my sister. Hadn't I often been jealous of her happy disposition, the way Mother smiled at her and frowned at me? And hadn't I felt angry that she had taken so easily to this new mother and had no thoughts of another? With shame I remembered all the times I had spoken impatiently to her and refused to play the games she liked best.

One afternoon, with my chores finished and Cynthia napping, I wandered aimlessly around, unable to think of anything to do.

"Why don't you get out your reticule and work on your quilt blocks?" Mother suggested.

I went to the trunk to find it. But when I saw Louvina's bag next to mine, tears suddenly welled up in my eyes and I couldn't touch it.

Instead I walked down to the river. Close to the water

I discovered a large bush with a few wild roses just beginning to bloom. They were so fresh and pink and sweet-smelling that I had to pick some. Carrying them back to camp, I put them in a pickle jar and set it down outside the tent.

As I was about to walk away, Father came to the opening.

"I think your sister may be breathing a little better," he said. "Would you heat up some milk, put in a pinch of soda, and bring it here?"

My feet practically flew over the ground as I ran to do what he asked. Crouched outside the tent door, I watched as Father lifted Louvina's head and tried to coax her to take some milk.

"I think she swallowed a drop or two," he told me.

The next morning Louvina opened her eyes and seemed to know where she was, though she still could not speak. Hope began to spring up in all of us. We gathered outside the tent. I was singing softly to Cynthia, and from inside we could hear Father humming a line from one of his favorite hymns: "Earth Has No Sorrow That Heaven Cannot Heal." A minute later he stepped outside and smiled at me.

"Louvina seems to be enjoying your roses," he said.

My heart leaped with joy and thankfulness as I hurried back to the wagon to help Mother prepare food for her. What did I care if I burned my fingers trying to make the toast? Surely now Louvina was going to get well.

Two days later Father bathed her, dressed her in clean, fresh clothes, and carried her to the improvised bed we had made for her on the two splint-bottomed chairs. Then he set to work, disinfecting the tent and scrubbing her clothes and his own.

As I walked back and forth from the river, carrying brimming pails of water for the washtub, I discovered more and more rose bushes. All of them were bursting with blooms. And each one seemed prettier to me than the last. I set down my pail. Picking as many roses as I could carry, I brought them back to Louvina.

She was sitting in the shade of the wagon, propped up with pillows, her doll tucked into bed beside her. Her cheeks, I noticed, had a little hint of color.

"See what I found," I said, holding out my armload of flowers.

Smiling weakly, Louvina reached out and buried her face in them.

"Oh, Sister!" she said, "aren't they pretty roses?"

Ten

It was only a few days more before Louvina was well enough for us to move on. Mother fixed up a bed for her in the wagon. I was eager to make up for all the times I had refused to play with her. Giving up my walking, I read out loud to her and invented new games with our dolls to amuse her. Every day she seemed to grow stronger. Soon she was sitting up and laughing, and we were sewing on our quilt blocks together.

The long rest had done our animals good. Their tender feet and sore shoulders had healed, and they moved along easily. Walking in the deeply rutted road, the oxen needed only Father's voice and an occasional snap of his whip to guide them. So he was able to ride and get some much-needed rest too.

All the way up the Platte we had encountered brief, hard thunderstorms that pelted us with rain and hail until the wagon cover was drenched, and dampness drifted down on us like mist. So we were not surprised one afternoon when the sky suddenly turned dark, and thunder muttered threateningly in the distance. But within a few minutes the sky was as black as midnight. Rain fell in pounding sheets, and thunder shook the earth beneath us as if it would tear it apart.

"Hold on to Buck!" I heard Father shouting to John.

The men had unhitched the oxen from the wagons and were holding them by the horns to keep the frightened animals from running away.

Already rain had soaked all the way through the wagon cover. The wind was shaking our wagon so hard, flapping and shrieking, that it seemed it might blow away like a tumbling leaf. Louvina and I held onto each other, our clothes dripping wet. But we were not as wet as Father and John, standing out in the storm.

I could barely make out their hunched figures, talking to the oxen.

"Easy now, Ben."

"Steady, Buck."

Then a blinding shaft of light came down out of the sky and struck the Grants' wagon. I saw it run around the iron rim of a wheel like a great ball of fire.

"What is it?" gasped Louvina.

"Lightning," answered Mother, her voice steady and calm.

Cynthia whimpered in her arms. Instinctively Louvina and I moved closer to her, huddling against Mother's damp skirts as more thunder crashed, and lightning stabbed the darkness with long knives of white. Never had I felt so wet and scared. Yet there was something comforting about us all being there together, gathered around Mother as if taking shelter beneath the branches of a tall unbending tree.

At last the thunder faded to a distant rumble. The rain became only a steady *drip, drip*. And when I looked outside again, the sun was breaking through the clouds.

Father and John were soaked through, and all of the animals looked bedraggled. But everyone was safe. We soon discovered, however, that the wagons were standing in two feet of water. The men had to drive the reluctant oxen back into all that water, hitch them up, and pull us out. It took a whole day to dry out Father's clothes.

The next afternoon we passed Chimney Rock, a tall stone spire that rose abruptly out of the plains into the sky. To me it looked like a church steeple pointing to heaven. And soon after that we were in Wyoming. The soil seemed different now, the roads more rocky than sandy, and the country was beginning to look more mountainous.

Ever since Mr. Grant had killed his first antelope, he kept going out on hunting expeditions, full of hope and determination. We all had a longing for fresh meat, having grown thoroughly tired of our usual diet of bacon, gravy, bread, and molasses. But the antelope were so fleet of foot that a horse had little chance of overtaking them. In a sudden burst of speed they would bound away, heads held high, white rumps disappearing in a cloud of dust. So Mr. Grant usually returned tired and discouraged.

One afternoon, after we had made an early camp, he decided to go out into the nearby low hills in search of game. Mounting his horse, he waved cheerfully to his family and rode away. Mealtime came, and Mr. Grant did not come back. Darkness began to settle over the camp, and still he did not appear.

Mrs. Grant and David came to our campfire.

"What could have happened to him?" Mrs. Grant

asked. Her small, thin face looked pinched, and her eyes were bright with worry.

Father tried to reassure her. "Perhaps he killed some game as evening was coming on," he suggested. "He would have to carry it on his horse and walk in, and that would take time."

David, who usually didn't say very much, spoke up then. His voice shook a little, but his dark eyes were determined. "I think I should go out and look for him."

Father looked at him with sympathy but shook his head. "It is too late for that. You would only get lost in the dark yourself. We must wait until morning."

He lit the Grants' lantern and our own, and hung them up as a guide for Mr. Grant to find our camp in the darkness. The lanterns burned all night, but in the morning he still had not come.

At daybreak, when Father went out to saddle his horse, he discovered Mr. Grant's horse, still saddled, grazing with the others. His eyes were grave as he walked back to our wagon.

"We are going to have to go out and look for him," he told Mother.

After a hurried breakfast Father and David Grant set off into the hills together. Each of them carried a canteen of water, lunch, and a small bottle of stimulant. They trailed Mr. Grant's horse behind them.

If only, I thought as I watched them ride away, that horse could talk and tell them which way to go.

John had been left behind to take care of the stock and watch over the rest of us. From the way he strode around, hands on his hips, hat pushed back on his head, I could tell he was feeling his importance as the only man in camp.

John had changed in the time since we left Arkansas, I realized suddenly. Although he was still thin, he had filled out in some way that I couldn't quite put my finger on. His arms and legs seemed a better match for his body now. There was a little swagger of confidence in his walk. Even his voice had begun to settle into a deeper register.

As soon as Father and David left, Mother and Mrs. Grant brought out their large wooden washtubs and tried to keep busy doing a washing. But all of us kept stopping every few minutes to peer into the bright distance, watching and waiting.

Noon came, and they had not returned. A merciless sun beat down, forcing us to seek shelter in the shade of the wagons. Mother and Mrs. Grant took out their mending, while Louvina and Cynthia played with a yarn ball. Idly I picked up Father's whip and tried again to crack it the way he did. But it was still too heavy for me. Disappointed, I put it down and went to get my sewing.

I could hear Mother talking, going on about nothing.

"That boy has done it again. Just look at the tear in this shirt. I tell you, I don't know how I'm going to keep him in clothes the way he is going. He'll wind up wearing rags before we're through."

She talked on and on, about biscuit recipes and the latest words Cynthia was learning to say. I knew she was trying to distract Mrs. Grant and keep her from worrying.

Time crept slowly by. About midafternoon a train of six wagons passed near us. One man stopped to ask if we needed help, and Mother told him about Mr. Grant.

"If he's lost out there," the man said, waving his dusty black hat in a wide circle, "it ain't likely he'll ever be found."

Mrs. Grant nearly collapsed at that, and Mother had to help her to a chair in the shade of the wagon.

"Don't pay any attention to him, Martha," she said soothingly. "That man doesn't know Thomas. Why, he doesn't know anything at all."

The afternoon wore down into evening. John went to milk the cows and put out the salt that helped keep them from straying. The sun was beginning to set off to the west, lighting up the land with deep-pink and purple shadows. But today none of us was interested in beautiful sunsets. We squinted into the sun, still straining to see.

Just as the last rays of sun sank below the horizon, I climbed up on the still-warm tongue of our wagon to take a last look.

Dimly outlined against a distant hill, I thought I saw something moving. Was it just my imagination, or could it be real? I closed my eyes, then opened them and looked again.

"Yes," I said out loud. "It's men on horses!"

Everyone gathered to look.

"I think I see three horses," John said excitedly. "But one has no rider. No, wait. There is something on that horse too. Can it be a man all doubled up?"

Slowly the figures drew nearer. I could make out Father riding Polly and David Grant on his horse and the extra horse between them. Both Father and David seemed to be reaching toward a bundle on Mr. Grant's horse.

Minutes later they came riding into camp. I stared, my mouth falling open in disbelief. Mr. Grant was wrapped up in Father's coat, his eyes so bleary and his face so purple and swollen that I hardly recognized him.

"Get his bed ready," ordered Father. "Quick!"

He and David lifted down the limp, hunched form and carried it to the Grants' tent.

"Thomas!" cried Mrs. Grant, reaching out her hand.

He tried to reply, but all that came out was a muffled groan.

In a few minutes Mr. Grant was settled into bed, his worn shoes and torn clothing removed. Very gently Mrs. Grant washed his face, and she and Father fed him spoonfuls of medicine and hot milk. After a time he fell into a feverish sleep.

"Will he be all right?" Mother asked in a hushed voice when Father finally returned to our wagon.

"They will likely be up with him most of the night," he replied. "He needs nourishment, and the fever must be kept down. With care, he should recover. But if we had not found him when we did, he surely would have died."

While Mother fixed him some supper, Father described how they had found Mr. Grant.

"He was lying out in the sun near a small bush. As we approached, he waved his hands, but he could not speak. His lips and tongue were dark and swollen. I tried to give him a drink, but he couldn't even swallow. So we moved him into the shade of a bush. We let water drip onto his tongue and washed his face and hands. After a while we mixed a little stimulant into the water and let it run down his throat. By that time the sun was setting, and I knew we had to get him back to camp.

"It was difficult getting him on his horse, as he could not hold himself upright. Finally we wrapped my coat around him, tying the empty sleeves to the saddle horn. Then we rode on either side of him, trying to brace him up. We had to stop many times to give him water and tie him back into position, but finally we made it back to camp."

By this time Father's head was slumped over and his words slurred with weariness.

"That is enough for now," Mother said. "You must get some rest. We can talk more in the morning."

In the morning Mr. Grant was still groaning with fever and exhaustion. Mrs. Grant and Mother took turns caring for him all day, feeding him and bathing his face with cool cloths, and by evening he was able to speak a little. The second day he was so much better that Father decided to move on, with Mr. Grant lying down in his wagon. And by the morning of the third day he was able to talk about his terrible experience, sitting in an easy chair near the campfire.

"After I had gone several miles out of camp," he began, "I spotted some antelope in the distance. I kept following them, hoping to get a shot, but I never came within range. I had just reached the top of a hill when I noticed that the sun was beginning to set. I was about to turn back when I saw a small herd of buffalo grazing just below me. To get a sure shot, I decided to tie my horse to a bush and creep up closer to them. But just as I was about to fire, an old bull put up his head and bellowed.

"I fired anyway but missed. The herd thundered away and was gone. And when I looked for my horse, it was gone too. It had pulled up the bush and run away.

"By now the sun had gone down. I caught a glimpse of my horse climbing a hill in the distance. I knew I needed that horse and the canteen of water it was carrying, so I put my gun under my arm and started running. But

I couldn't catch up to it. After a time I realized that I was only tiring myself out and getting nowhere, and I was becoming very thirsty.

"It grew dark, and I was no longer sure which way to walk. I tried to tell direction by the lay of the land and the position of the stars overhead, but I began to feel lost. I was so thirsty and the gun was so heavy. Finally I just had to stop and rest.

"But soon I was roused by the howling of wolves. Knowing that I dared not lie there any longer, I walked on. The gun was a burden, but I knew I might soon need it, so I clutched it and staggered along. The stars and the Dipper looked strange in the sky. I didn't know which way to go. After a while I could walk no more, so I gathered some dry grasses and a few twigs and made a small fire. In the firelight I could see the glowing yellow eyes of those wolves all around me. I fired a shot in their direction and kept my fire burning. It was a long night.

"When daylight came, the wolves slunk away. I began to walk again, thinking I would soon come to something that looked familiar. But nothing did. I was suffering from terrible thirst and weariness. I wanted to give up, but my burning thirst urged me on. The sun was cooking me to my very bones. My throat felt choked, and there seemed to be a tight ring around my head. Somehow I managed to stagger on until afternoon, and then could go no farther. I tried to crawl to the shade of a little bush. And there I lay until you found me."

Telling his story seemed to have exhausted Mr. Grant again. He sagged back in his chair. Everyone else was quiet.

I thought about how Mr. Grant must have felt, lying

helpless and all alone out in those hills. What an awful, desperate feeling it would be, wondering if you would ever be found. And I thought about how much our animals meant to us, and those precious drops of water, and having each other.

Then, very softly, Father began to sing a hymn of praise. Mother joined in, and then the rest of us.

"Hallelujah!" we sang.

At that Mr. Grant tried to join in too. His face was still swollen and haggard, and his voice trembled. But his eyes were shining with thankfulness.

Eleven

For some time now we had been crossing the Rocky Mountains. But most of the time the inclines had been so gradual that we hardly realized it. From the very beginning of our journey, Father told us, we actually had been climbing—across the vast prairies, up hills and down and up once more. Now we could see tall rocky peaks in the distance, scraping up against the clouds.

It was the middle of July, two weeks later than Father had hoped, when we passed Fort Laramie. I was disappointed that we didn't even catch a glimpse of the fort. Once it had been a trading post of the Hudson's Bay Company, but now the main road passed it by. And soon after that we left the Platte River at last. We had followed it for over four hundred miles, Father said. It seemed to me like much more.

Now we had to cross fifty miles of desert, covered only by sagebrush and a few dried-up, salt-crusted ponds, to reach the banks of the Sweetwater River. On the first day we made twenty-two miles, starting early in the morning and traveling late into the evening until we reached a place called Willow Springs. In all that time we did not pass a single stream. We weren't thirsty, since we carried kegs of water with us, but our animals suffered. John and I gave Polly and Rover a small drink each. And Mr. Grant, remembering his terrible experience in the wilderness, felt so sorry for his animals that he tried to give every one of them a little water. But the small amount only seemed to increase their thirst.

Another long day's journey brought us to the Sweetwater, a cool, clear, fast-running stream with flowers dotting its banks. And the day after that we passed through the Devil's Gate. Here the river had worn its way through a tiny gap between mountains that stood four hundred feet high. To me it looked as if some giant's hand had sawn apart those mountains just far enough for a stream to wind through.

Now we were really in the Rockies. I could understand how they had gotten their name. Tall spires of rock towered up on every side, with very little growing on them except in places where dirt and sand had been blown into small crevices. Here and there I saw white gleams of snow. A little farther on, Father said, we would come to South Pass, where the waters divided.

"It is called the Continental Divide," he explained. "Every drop of water in one stream will flow toward the Atlantic Ocean, and in the next, every drop of water will flow to the Pacific."

Standing next to him in the chilly morning air, looking at a ragged patch of snow up on the mountainside, I felt myself shiver. All of these mountains still to cross, I thought. And snow coming before too long. It came early in the mountains, I knew from all the stories we had heard. Pulling Mother's shawl close around me, I hurried to gather wood for a bonfire.

But a few days later, just beyond South Pass, we found ourselves crossing another desert.

"This one looks to be about forty miles wide," Father told us, after carefully studying his guidebook. "And no water to be found until we reach the Green River on the other side."

Although Mr. Grant's strength was quickly returning, his ordeal seemed to have made him more cautious.

"It would not be wise to try to cross in the heat of the day," he warned.

So we filled up every bucket and keg and cooking pot and any other vessel that would hold water, and at four o'clock that afternoon we started out.

Even this late in the day the sun felt fiery hot. Within an hour the oxen were all panting, their long pink tongues lolling out. We stopped to give them a short rest and to eat our cold supper of dried meat and bread. Picking up a bucket of water, John went to each of the oxen, washing the dust off their noses and letting them wet their tongues.

All that night, under a pale sliver of moon, the wagons rumbled along, bumping over sagebrush and gravel beds and slogging through sand. Father and Mr. Grant walked alongside, cracking their whips and calling out to the oxen.

"Get up, Ben."

"Gee a little there, Jerry."

Louvina and Cynthia slept through all the noise, but I kept waking up. The shouts and the popping of whips rang in my ears. And that clatter of the wheels that never stopped. No longer did they seem to be saying, "Going-to-Oregon. Going-to-Oregon." Instead they just whispered softly, "Chuggety-chug. Chuggety-chug. Chuggety-chug." Sometimes I felt as if all I had ever done was ride in this wagon, and those wheels were going to keep on turning forever.

At last, about noon of the following day, we came out of the desert into the cool shade of the Green River. The last few miles were down a steep rocky slope. The oxen were so glad to see water that Father could barely stop them from running right into the river.

I felt almost the same. I dipped my hands into the clear icy water, splashed some on my face, then let it run through my fingers until they tingled with the delicious cold.

"Look over there," Mother said, bending down next to me.

Growing close to the water were clumps of sour dock and other weeds.

"Oh, can we pick some?" I asked.

For weeks now I had been pining for green vegetables and fruits. We occasionally got fresh meat, making a change from our usual bread and bacon, and Blackie still gave a little milk. And almost every Sunday we had a mess of dried fruit. But that was not the same.

"Yes," said Mother, with one of her rare smiles.

She and I gathered them up and fixed greens for supper, and everyone ate them happily.

All during our long trip through Wyoming we kept encountering wagon trains in far worse condition than we were. Many oxen had given out by now, and cows had to be put in their places in the teams. Some wagons had also given out, forcing families to double up. Food supplies were growing dangerously low, and many people were sick and discouraged. Occasionally some family still turned back.

"We're going back to God's country," one gaunt, sunken-eyed couple said to us, "if these critters will only take us there."

Father always stopped to help whenever he could. He assisted men in resetting tires and mending broken-down wagons. He and Mother insisted on sharing our food, even Blackie's small amount of milk. And he never seemed too tired to offer cheerful advice to families in distress.

"Thank you, Mr. Todd," they would say, eyes brimming with gratitude, and I felt a warm flush of pride at having such a father.

We often met Indians along the way. Sometimes we traded with them for buffalo meat, if it was fresh. Always they tried to tell us that they were peaceful toward the whites. Most recently it had been the Crows who would ride up to us, their faces brightly painted, and say, "Go fight Sioux." Yet we also kept hearing about their stealing stock from other wagon trains, especially horses and young cattle.

One morning John came back from tending the animals, his face looking troubled.

"Pet is missing," he told Father.

"Maybe she has only strayed a little," Father said.

He went out searching for the horse, but he could not find her.

"I am afraid she must have been taken by the Indians," Father told us when he returned. We had seen a few Indians in the distance the night before.

"Poor Pet," sighed Louvina, her eyes slowly filling up

with tears. The gray mare was nearly as tame as Daisy had been, and had learned to eat out of our hands.

For the next two days Louvina kept looking over her shoulder, peering out the back of the wagon as if she expected to see Pet come galloping to catch up with us. But we never saw her again.

On a morning soon after that we were traveling along as usual. We had gone about five or six miles when Father sent John on ahead to look for a nooning place. Louvina and I were walking at the back of the wagon. Up ahead I could see John stopping at what appeared to be a small creek. Just past him, up on a ridge, was an Indian camp.

As we came closer, I noticed that the Indians were packing up to leave, putting packs on ponies, strapping papooses to the women's backs. We had become so used to them by now that I didn't think anything about it.

But suddenly about twenty of those Indians, some of them on horseback, rushed toward John. They were shouting and shaking their buffalo robes at him, trying to stampede his horse. Polly reared up on her hind legs. John cried out, and I saw them surround him.

"What is this?" Father said sharply, urging the oxen forward.

Moments later Indian ponies blocked the path of our wagons. People and animals milled about in confusion.

A young Indian on horseback came circling back, a rope in his hand, his long black hair and blanket streaming in the wind. Before I knew what was happening, he had thrown a lasso at me.

I stared in stunned surprise as it struck the wagon cover above my head, then settled over me. I tried to throw it off, but I could feel the rope slipping down over my hands.

The Indian was so close. His black eyes glittered.

"No!" I cried under my breath.

I struggled with the rope. I had to get it off. I had to get away from that Indian.

Then somehow I had fought my way free. Louvina and I scrambled desperately into our wagon. Quickly I buttoned down the cover. As I did, I caught a glimpse of another Indian cutting the rope that tied Blackie to the back of the wagon.

It was so dark inside, I could see nothing. But I heard John screaming at the top of his lungs as he fought with the Indians. Other Indians were struggling with Father, probably trying to take away his gun, I thought. I heard a grunt, a cry of pain, then a dull thud. Cynthia was sobbing in a low, ragged voice. More shouts and sounds of scuffling came from the Grants' wagon behind us.

It was clear that we were surrounded, and outnumbered too. Yet for some reason the Indians hesitated to finish off the attack.

Then I felt something poke at the wagon cover right beside me. An Indian was trying to lift it, to see what was inside. But why? Did they want to see how many more were in our party, to make sure they really outnumbered us? Louvina and I held on to each other, too frightened to speak. I could barely breathe. The wagon cover was jabbed again, from the other side this time. Luckily I had fastened it tight.

Several more times this happened. The Indians seemed to have decided that they had nothing to fear from us. They were closing in. Their shouts grew louder, turning into war whoops. This was the end. At any moment now they would attack. I closed my eyes, my hand gripping Louvina's tightly.

Just then a shot was fired nearby.

The Indians grew suddenly silent. I heard another shot. A moment later hoofbeats pounded away, fading into the distance.

"They're gone!" cried Mother. Her voice cracked, turning into a sob.

I couldn't believe it. What had happened to drive them away? I crawled to the opening in the wagon cover. It was true. All of those Indians had disappeared, vanished like smoke. And then I understood why. To our rear, up on a small ridge, I could make out a party of three or four hunters. Behind them was a broad cloud of dust that could only be another wagon train.

Louvina and I laughed with relief. Mother was crying. John seemed to be half-laughing and half-crying as he told the story of how the Indians had forced him off his horse. Putting down his rifle, Father went to comfort Mother. As I took Cynthia out of Mother's arms, tears were streaming down her plump cheeks.

"Don't yike them," she sobbed, clinging to my neck.

We were relieved to find Blackie quietly grazing a short distance away. And soon the hunters came riding up: one lean and gray-haired and weather-beaten, another big with an easy smile, and a boy about John's age.

"We heard you shouting and saw the Indians," the older one said, his blue eyes bright against leathery brown skin. "We figured something must be wrong, so we fired our guns."

"Thank you!" was all Father and Mother and the Grants could say, over and over again.

When the rest of their long wagon train caught up with us, Father talked to its captain, a man named Joab Powell. He agreed to take us under his protection.

We had not seen such a large wagon train, with so many people and vast herds of cattle and horses, since our first days out from Independence. That night all of the wagons were arranged in a circle. The tongue of one was attached to the rear wheels of the next, forming a kind of fence. Inside this tight safe corral were all our animals, the horses securely picketed to stakes, and ourselves. And Captain Powell posted guards in shifts, to keep watch for Indians all night long.

"Will they come back?" asked Louvina, when at last we were putting on our nightclothes. Her eyes were big in the lamplight, and her fingers clutched at the neck of her nightgown.

"I don't think so," Father reassured her. "It is not that those Indians were on the warpath with the whites. They just saw a small party and thought they could overpower us and make off with our animals. But now that we are part of a large wagon train, I believe we are safe."

I couldn't stop thinking about that young Indian who had thrown his lasso at me.

"If he had caught me, would he have dragged me away?" I asked Father.

Father was silent for a moment, and his voice was sober when he replied. "We can't know for certain what he would have done. But remember: 'I will fear no evil: for thou art with me.' Good night, Mary Ellen. Try to go to sleep now."

I wrapped myself in Grandma's quilt, trying to put aside the troubling pictures all jumbled inside my head so I could sleep. Little by little the evening sounds of camp grew quiet. Fires died out and everyone but the guards went off to bed. I could hear a low indistinct murmur of talk from the next wagon. A horse gave a muffled whinny. A touch of breeze rustled the wagon cover for a moment, then moved away. Somewhere far off a wolf howled.

At that, dogs began to bark. Large dogs and little dogs. Deep baying voices and shrill yapping ones. And Rover's familiar growl.

If any Indians tried to sneak up on this camp, I thought sleepily, surely they would be frightened away.

Twelve

"What's the matter with those men?" Louvina whispered in my ear.

"Which men?" I asked, looking around.

I was finding so much to stare at inside the high walls of Fort Hall. There was the fort itself, built of sunbaked adobe, with a wide, square dirt yard in the middle. And the people: a few soldiers in uniform, some whiskery rough-looking mountain men, Indians belonging to the Snake and Shoshone tribes, so we'd been told, and small groups of travelers like ourselves, stopped to shoe horses and trade for food and supplies. But the thing I couldn't keep my eyes away from was the houses facing the square. Solid walls and doors and windows. And inside, most likely, tables spread with cloths and cupboards filled with china dishes, and real bedsteads.

With a little twinge of pain, like a toothache that kept returning, I thought again of our house back in Arkansas. Mother's roses blooming next to the front door. A friendly curl of smoke rising from the chimney. That put me in mind of the meetinghouse and the schoolhouse and how much I had been missing my studies. I had a sudden sharp longing to forget about Oregon, wherever it was, and stay right here.

"*Those* men!" Louvina nudged me, pointing and giggling. "They look so funny."

Two men in buckskin breeches were leading their horses toward the blacksmith. Though they were standing up, their breeches curved as if they were sitting down.

"It's not polite to point, Louvina," Father corrected her gently. But he too had to smile. "It looks as if they were out in the damp and let their clothes dry while they were seated."

We had come from camp a mile away to buy extra linchpins for the wagon, as well as crackers, sugar, and maybe a little fresh milk. Our cow Lillie had died three days ago from eating a poison weed. Mother, who seemed always tired now, was resting back in camp with Cynthia.

"You girls stay close to me," Father told us.

Drinking in the rich smells of smoked meat, fish, tobacco, fur skins, the red-hot iron of the blacksmith's fire, Louvina and I trailed after Father as he traded for the things we needed. Afterward, my hands clutching a half-full pail of milk, we waited while he talked with Captain Powell and some other men in the cool shadows of the yard.

Their voices buzzed on. The sun began to sink in the sky, and long shadows came creeping across the yard. I watched a small group of Indian women and children nearby. They were dressed in deerskin decorated with red ribbons and porcupine quills and beads of many colors, and the women wore shiny brass bracelets on their arms and rings on their fingers. The colors were bright against their dark-brown skin and glossy black hair. They appeared friendly to me. Looking at a girl about my age playing with a fat baby, I wished suddenly that we spoke the same language so I could talk to her.

"It is settled then," I heard Father say, shaking hands with a giant of a man who had a bushy graying beard.

"We pull out at first light tomorrow," replied the man in a deep voice.

That is how we learned that we were leaving Captain Powell's wagon train to join a smaller one led by this man, Captain Clark.

"Why?" I asked Father on our way back to camp. I had felt so safe in Captain Powell's company, closed inside that big circle of wagons every night with so many rifles to protect us.

"It is because of Mother," Father answered, not quite looking at me. "You know she has not been feeling very well. A smaller train can move faster and get us to Oregon sooner. Also, in a smaller train if one of the families should have to stop, the rest will not go on without them."

Something strange in his voice made me stop and take notice. What was the matter with Mother? I wondered. Was she not just tired from traveling but truly sick? And was Father so concerned about her that he thought we might have to stop?

Of course. The moment I saw her back in camp, rubbing her back as she straightened up from bending over the fire, I knew what it was. Mother was not sick. She was going to have a baby. Why hadn't I realized it weeks ago? I had seen other women with thickening waists, their faces pale and their eyes weary from too many miles of jouncing in the wagons. And I had seen wagons suddenly halted along the trail so a baby could be born. Just a few nights ago, in fact, Mother and Mrs. Grant had gone to try to help a young woman in the Powell train who was having a difficult birth. I had heard them return very late, and Mother say to Father in a hollow voice, "She worked so hard. But the baby was born dead."

A new baby. The idea unfurled in my mind like an opening flower. We were going to have a brand-new baby in our family. Maybe it would be a boy this time. Father would like that. He was always telling people jokingly that he was "surrounded by females." Louvina didn't know about the baby yet and neither, of course, did Cynthia. Only I did. It was a secret, I thought with a little rush of pleasure, that I shared with Mother.

Then I remembered the young woman whose baby had been born dead. That couldn't happen to Mother. This baby—our baby—was going to be born healthy and strong. I would help make it so, I promised myself, by taking care of Mother. I would do more of the chores at mealtimes so she could rest, and carry things so she wouldn't have to bend over. Smiling to myself, I went to lift the biscuit pan out of the fire.

Just after dawn the next day our wagon and the Grants' fell in behind the eight others of the Clark train. And the bright walls of Fort Hall, like all the other landmarks and campsites that in my mind's eye stretched out in a line going east all the way to Independence, faded slowly to nothing in the distance.

Though large and powerful like the mountains around us, Captain Clark was quiet and easy in his ways. His wife, cheerful and tiny with birdlike bones, talked more than he did. Traveling with them was his sister, Mrs. McReynolds, a widow who had lost her husband along the trail. In her eyes I could see a glaze of grief, but she traveled along steadily and quietly, seeming determined to finish the journey they had started together. And there were about five McReynolds and four Clark children, who were in and out of each other's wagons so much that they all mixed together in my mind.

Soon we came to the Snake River, a wandering greenish stream cut so deep into rock that in many places we could only look at it, not get down to drink from it. We were to follow this river for the next three hundred miles. We passed the American Falls, a beautiful tumbling torrent of water fifty feet high, and a few miles farther, the Raft River. Here the trail that led to California veered off to the left.

"The Tedrose party was headed that way, the store-keeper at Fort Hall told me," Father said.

I thought of Sarah Jane, trudging beside her wagon up that shallow valley toward a far-off mountain peak. Our ways had parted once again.

For several days after that we traveled across dry, desolate country. As far as my eyes could see was nothing but hot yellow sand and gray sagebrush. I gathered up the dry brush for Mother's fires, but it burned with a smell that was worse than buffalo chips. The sun scorched the top of our heads. Dust flew in clouds. Sometimes from up on the spring seat we could see neither Father nor the team. At night, if we managed to find a camping place that had both water and a little grass, we were thankful. And if there were a few sticks of wood for a fire as well, we positively rejoiced.

Our oxen were growing so thin that their bones stood out like sharp mountain ridges. Buck and Ben looked at Father with reproachful eyes as he yoked them to the wagon each morning. Louvina and I felt so sorry for them that we tried to think of some way to help.

One day, as the two of us were walking along next to the wagon, I spotted a little clump of green ahead.

"Look, Louvina," I said, pointing.

"Grass!" she cried joyfully.

She raced ahead and began pulling it up in big bunches. I ran after her. When we had all we could carry, we walked back and held out handfuls of grass to Buck and Ben.

"Go on, have some," offered Louvina.

Oxen could not smile. It was silly to think they could. But there was something close to it in their mild, dark eyes as they chewed gratefully on that sweet, soft grass.

For days after that we gathered every little blade of grass we could find in our aprons and fed it to the oxen as we traveled along.

Now illness came to our wagon train again. It began with two of Mrs. McReynolds' children, fifteen-year-old Rebecca and twelve-year-old George, who were stricken with mountain fever. They had aching muscles and rashes and high fevers. Soon some of the Clark children, as well as others in the train, also had the sickness. It struck suddenly, and sometimes the fever rose so high that the victim would rave in delirium.

Remembering Louvina's brush with death on the banks of the Platte, I felt a little pinch of fear. Would this sickness be as terrible as the cholera had been? But we could not stop moving. It was now past the middle of August, and the men were beginning to worry about being snowbound in the mountains that lay ahead. Mrs. McReynolds had all she could do taking care of her sick children, so everyone else tried to help her in any way they could. Jesse, who at nineteen was the oldest of the Clark children and a thinner, darker copy of his father, drove her wagon. And John took care of her loose stock.

As the country became rougher and rockier, more and more oxen were giving out. Footsore, weary, and weak with hunger, they would lie down and nothing could get them up again. They had to be left behind.

"We need to lighten the load for the animals we have left," Captain Clark told the company one evening. Four more oxen had been lost that day, and the strain showed on his deeply lined face. "I must ask each of you to remove as much weight as you possibly can from your wagons."

Some cut down their wagon beds. Others took out camp stoves and rocking chairs, spinning wheels and chests and cooking pots. We left a trunk with most of Mother's good china and her pretty handwoven tablecloths sitting beside the trail.

One man, Mr. Judson, set out a heavy wooden rolling pin, then snatched it up again.

"Do I really need to throw this away?" he asked Father. I was amazed to see tears actually rolling down his cheeks. "It was my mother's. I remember she always used it to roll out her biscuits. And they were awful good biscuits."

Father looked at him, a big stout man with a face like a little boy. "Anything that we can do without will make a difference," he said gently.

So the rolling pin too was left behind.

At a place called Salmon Falls Captain Clark brought our wagon train to a halt again. A decision had to be made about which trail to follow. The main road went along the south side of the Snake River, but the grass there looked to be scarce. Captain Clark thought we might do better by crossing to the other side.

Some of the other men disagreed with him. I heard Father and Mr. Grant discussing it that evening.

"We should stick to the old road," Mr. Grant argued. "It is bound to be faster."

"But so many have traveled it before us. What if there is no grass?" questioned Father. "We can't afford to lose any more oxen."

The men talked about it for hours. Finally they took a vote. It turned out that everyone except Captain Clark and Father favored following the old road. The other men felt so strongly about it that the next morning they told Captain Clark they had decided to split from the train.

"Come with us," Mr. Grant urged Father. Since his experience in the wilderness, his body seemed to have shrunk inside his frayed and faded clothes, but his eyes still flashed with feeling. "You know how dangerous any delay is now. You cannot run the risk."

He was talking about the mountain snows. But I thought of Mother and the baby that would soon be born.

Father hesitated. A struggle seemed to be going on somewhere behind his calm clear eyes.

"We cannot leave the Clarks alone," he said finally. "Not with all the sickness they've had. We must stay with them."

So once again we parted with old friends.

Mr. Grant waved a smiling farewell, a trace of the old bounce in his steps as he hitched up his oxen. But Mother's shoulders seemed to sag as she said good-bye to Mrs.

Grant, pressing into her hand a gift of flower seeds from her garden. And it was strange to see John heading out to herd the cattle without David at his side. Though my eyes saw it, my mind couldn't quite accept that this was happening. We had been with the Grants so long, I had begun to think we would always be together, even in Oregon.

"Good-bye!" Our voices echoed in the thin morning air.

And once again I felt that empty, lonesome feeling as I watched the Grants' wagon, its cover now a dull and dusty gray, roll slowly out of sight.

After crossing the river, we found ourselves in a pretty, grassy valley. It was like a wild meadow, only little hills jutted up here and there, the rye grass was tall, and springs babbled out of the rocky walls on the north side. Captain Clark stopped the wagons, and he and Father smiled at each other. All that day we rested, taking care of the sick children, enjoying the cool water, and letting the animals graze on all that good grass until they had their fill. Watching Buck and Ben, big clumps of green dripping from their mouths, I wished we could stay there for a long time.

But of course the next day we had to move on. As we followed the path of the river, we began to encounter Indians who were also suffering from sickness. However their sickness was not mountain fever, Father said. It was smallpox. To treat the disease the Indians put the sick person in a tepee on the banks of the river. Hot rocks were placed all around and hot drinks given, until a sweat was produced. Then the victim was plunged into the cold river. The treatment did not seem to be working, as Indians were dying there by the dozens.

One day we found a nooning place on a flat, sandy bank of the river. I was wandering around, chewing on a dry crust of bread, when I saw John walk over to a deserted tepee. Curious, I followed him.

"Don't look, Mary Ellen!" John warned, turning suddenly to block me from going in.

But I had already glimpsed what was inside: a pile of dead Indians stacked up like logs, their hands and feet sticking out from under a tattered buffalo robe.

"Oh!" I cried, dropping my bread in horror.

Blindly I ran for the wagon. Through the tall, stinging grass I raced, tripping and stumbling. And then—what was that lying in the grass right in front of me? It couldn't be, but it was. Another dead Indian! I was running so fast now I couldn't stop. Without looking, I leapt over it and kept on going.

A moment later I was pulling myself up into our wagon. I took refuge in its dim, comforting interior. My legs were trembling and my breath came in long ragged gasps. My heart was fluttering like a frightened bird.

"Are you all right, Mary Ellen?" Mother's face, pale and concerned, appeared at the opening in the wagon cover.

I nodded, not able to speak.

"Why don't you stay inside and work on your quilt pieces for a little while?" she suggested.

"All right," I whispered.

And there I stayed for the rest of the afternoon.

Some of the sick children were beginning to improve. But now Mrs. Clark had come down with the fever. I missed her bustling presence and her cheerful, encouraging voice around the cooking fires. Still, we kept moving as fast as we could.

Then one morning I woke up with chills. My body ached all over, and I couldn't get out of bed.

Mother felt my forehead. "It is the fever," she said.

Father gave me some medicine, but instead of feeling better, I felt even worse. All that day I huddled underneath my quilt on my feather bed, sometimes shivering, other times burning hot, while the wagon jolted along over steep, rough, rocky roads. In a kind of feverish dream I listened to the murmur of the wagon wheels.

Now they did not say "Going-to-Oregon" or even "Chuggety-chug, chuggety-chug." They didn't say anything at all. I kept wanting to cry out to them, "Stop! Let me rest!" But even in my dream I knew we could not stop.

In the evening Mother brought me a little gruel with cream in it. Looking at the bowl, I shook my head.

"Take just a little," she urged me. "It will make you stronger."

I made myself take a bite, but it didn't taste good. Weakly I pushed the spoon away.

The next few days went by in a haze. I slept and woke, took a sip of water or ate a few bites, then slept again. Mother's blurred face came and went, her eyes looking anxious, urging me to eat. Father often sat next to me, holding my hand in his big warm one. One morning, smiling, he told me that I had kept everyone awake in the night with my singing, though I did not remember it at all. He also said that I was not as sick as Mrs. Clark and some of the others.

But I did not want to get out of the wagon, or even

look out the opening at the blinding brightness of the sky. At night I had dreams, terrible confusing visions of wolves and wagons lying in broken pieces, oxen that kept walking even though they were only a strung-together collection of white bones, dead Indians stacked up in piles.

Once I dreamed that the young Indian with the glittering black eyes was throwing his lasso at me. The rope was closing around my neck. I kept screaming and trying to get into the wagon. But somehow its sides had suddenly grown as tall and steep as a cliff, so tall and steep that I could not climb them.

"Mary Ellen!"

My eyes opened to find Father bending over me.

"The Indian," I mumbled fearfully, not sure if I was asleep or awake. "He had a rope. He was trying to get me."

"No one is after you, honey," he reassured me. "You are safe here with Mother and Father. Don't cry now."

Father gave me a drink of water and bathed my face and hands with a cool cloth. Then very gently he stroked my hair, humming under his breath, "Oh, Happy Day."

His voice was so soothing and his touch so soft. Surely, I thought, my eyes beginning to close, my father must be the best man in the whole world. The image of that Indian's eyes slowly faded away. And I drifted off to sleep again.

Thirteen

It seemed like one more dream that my feverish brain had invented: the rising walls of another small fort, this one called Fort Boise and smelling overpoweringly of fish. Still another river crossing, with swiftly running water lapping hungrily at the sides of our wagon-bed boat, weakly bawling cattle, men shouting at the poor struggling oxen. And when the crossing was finally over, I heard the hushed, sad voices of Father and Mother on the other side of the wagon cover.

We would not see Mrs. Clark's cheery smile ever again. While we had been crossing the Snake, she had crossed over from life to death.

They buried her on the bank of the river. Father dug a shallow grave, and Mother looked everywhere for flowers to place on that bare mound of earth. All she could find were a few sunflowers, but they were pretty. She brought them to the wagon to show me.

From my bed I saw Jesse Clark pass by, holding the

hand of his five-year-old brother, Willie. Tears were rolling down both their faces. And a little later I heard far-off, faint voices singing a farewell hymn.

"Oh, Lamb of God," it ended, "I come, I come."

As soon as the wagons could be set up again and re-packed, we had to move on. Little Willie kept crying for his mother, so Mother brought him to our wagon to try to comfort him. I was able to sit up now, but I was still too weak to get out of the wagon. Louvina had to do all of my chores. She played with Willie and did the dishes and carried water from the river. While filling the water bucket that afternoon, she found wild peppermint growing along the riverbank, and Mother used it to brew some tea for me. I thought it tasted a little good.

Although I no longer had a fever, it seemed as if the bad dreams would not stop. Only I knew in my heart that I was not dreaming. Now it was Captain Clark who was sick with the fever. Though he struggled to keep leading the train, all the strength seemed suddenly to have drained out of this giant of a man. Finally he was forced to take to his bed.

Two days later our wagon was in the lead when suddenly I heard terrible screams coming from somewhere behind us.

"Whoa!" Father shouted to the oxen. Turning to Mother, he asked, "What was that?"

"I think it came from the Clark wagon," Mother told him. "You'd better go and see what has happened."

Father was gone for a long time. Later he told us about the dreadful scene he encountered when he reached the Clarks' wagon.

Captain Clark was out of bed, staggering around with

a butcher knife in his hand. Apparently he had tried to stab his son Jesse with it. The poor man was so out of his mind with fever and grief, Father said, that he did not know what he was doing. The younger children were screaming and sobbing, and little Willie had crawled under a flour sack, trying to hide himself from his father.

Father talked to Captain Clark until finally he calmed down and handed over the knife. Then he sent Jesse to drive our team and the trembling Willie to be soothed by Mother. He put Captain Clark to bed, and drove his wagon for the rest of the day.

For several days after that Captain Clark raved like a crazy man, and then he slipped into unconsciousness. Finally, he too died. He was buried beside another river, the Powder. And on the very day of his death his son Jesse was taken sick with the same fever.

Mrs. McReynolds took care of him and the other three Clark children and drove her own wagon, patient and uncomplaining. With her broad face and her blank expressionless eyes, she reminded me of the oxen, plodding along steadily without seeming to know anymore where she was going or why.

I looked at her and at little Willie, an orphan now, so silent and shrunk into himself that he seemed to grow smaller every day. And I wondered why. Why had the Clarks left their safe home back in Ohio to make this journey that had ended so tragically for them? And what about all those other families who had buried a child or a mother or father beside the Platte River? I had heard a hundred times, it seemed, all the reasons for setting out for Oregon: the free land, the wonderful climate, the riches to be found. But suddenly they no longer made sense. What good was any of that if people died?

And what about Father? He was a careful man, a sensible man, yet he also had put his family at risk. And when Mother was about to have a baby too. Feelings that had been simmering inside me for a long time—since Daisy died, or maybe even longer—came bubbling up. All at once I was furious with Father. How could he do that to us?

Then, for the first time in several weeks, Grandma's face floated into my mind. I could see her firm chin, her clear blue eyes, the energy that seemed always about to burst from her small body. She had done what we were doing now, and she had flourished. Maybe, I thought, it was some sort of spirit that was passed down from one generation to the next. An itch in the feet, or in the brain. A feeling of dissatisfaction, of thinking always that things could be better. Or maybe something even simpler: the need to look over the next mountain and see what was on the other side. Whatever it was, it seemed to run in our family. I wondered if, like Grandma and Father, I would ever have it too.

Now there was no one but Father to lead our little wagon train.

We left the Snake River, and for a time followed Burnt River, a small stream that wandered through deep-cut canyons. After miles of nothing but sagebrush we began to see scattered junipers, and beyond them, in the distance, trees. These were the first forests we had seen since we left Missouri.

It was well into September by now. The nights were beginning to grow cold as we approached the Blue Mountains. I could see my breath in the frosty air as I got dressed in the early mornings. We put on extra coats and built our campfires bigger. Still, Cynthia's hands and feet were sometimes so cold that she cried.

The Blue Mountains were even steeper and rockier than the Rockies. Up and up we climbed for three long days. Up sharp-pitched rises and along narrow ridges, over rock-filled streams, and in and out of hollows. The oxen were so worn out that they had to be goaded to start, but once started, they strained and kept pulling. And then down slopes so steep that the wagon brakes had to be set on the last notch, and the wheels locked with chains besides. Sometimes it seemed as if the heavy wagons would run over the poor patient beasts.

All around us now were trees. Most of them were evergreens, tall and straight and spicy-smelling. They rose into the air like dark columns, standing so close together that their branches intertwined. At last we could gather enough wood for our campfires. And we needed it. Cold winds whistled in the treetops. We had rain, and one morning a little snow.

One afternoon after we had stopped to make camp, Mother mixed up a pan of bread dough. She set it out on a fallen log to rise, then went on with her work. From my perch up on the wagon seat I saw Buck, one of our lead oxen, come wandering back into camp.

"Mother!" I called. "The bread!"

Mother hurried toward the log, John right behind her. "Shoo, Buck!" he cried.

But it was too late. Buck's big black nose was in the pan. The bread dough dangled out of his mouth in sticky white strings.

"Buck! Come back!"

John chased after him, shouting and waving his arms.

Mother just stood there, as straight and still as one of the trees, not saying a word. Her eyes glistened with tears. I knew how little flour we had left to carry us through.

A few minutes later John came back. "I'm sorry," he said. "I couldn't get it out of his mouth."

Mother looked at him blankly. Then, unexpectedly, the corners of her mouth twitched.

"If you had gotten it out of his mouth," she said, smiling, "what would you have done with it?"

John looked at Mother a little sheepishly, and we all started to laugh.

Good old Buck, I thought. We were sure to suffer from the loss of that precious flour. But he did deserve a treat.

Coming down the long, jolting slope from the Blue Mountains, we found ourselves in prairie land once again, with willows and cottonwood trees, and another river to follow, the Umatilla. We made camp close by it. Here we encountered more Indians, this time of the Cayuse tribe. They seemed peaceful and industrious, doing some farming and even a little gardening.

I was finally strong enough to help out again. Walking to the river for water that evening, I stumbled upon an Indian garden. It was only a small plot, with more bare stalks and yellowing vines than anything else. But there, growing out of the dark rich soil, was a large cabbage.

It had been so long since I had seen any vegetables growing. I stood still, gazing at that cabbage with a kind of wonder. It was so green, so leafy and fresh. My mouth watered longingly. In my mind I could almost taste it.

"Mary Ellen!"

I turned to find Father watching me.

"You know you mustn't touch it," he said quietly, his steady gray eyes holding mine.

Of course I knew he was right. It was just that I was so hungry for green things. Only the night before I had been gnawing on a twig torn from a tree.

"No, sir," I said.

I couldn't let myself look again. Turning my back on that cabbage, I walked quickly away.

Father tried to buy vegetables from the Indians, but they shook their heads at him. They had only enough for themselves. Instead they offered to sell him chokecherries. But we had never tried them, and Mother was worried that they might be poisonous. So we had to go on, my awful craving for vegetables and fruits still unsatisfied.

When I awoke the next morning, I heard a strange little cry. It sounded like a bird, I thought groggily, or some other small creature.

Opening my eyes, I saw Father looking down at me. On his face was a broad smile.

"I have a surprise for you," he said.

Louvina and Cynthia were already awake, chattering about what the surprise could be. Father pushed aside the blanket curtain, and the three of us stared.

A new baby was in bed with Mother.

She was smiling too, though her face was as pale as the pillow cover and dark circles of exhaustion ringed her eyes. Weakly she drew back the blanket so my sisters and I could see.

The baby was so tiny and pink and helpless-looking. It had a red, squashed-in face and a worried look, like an old person. On top of its head was a funny dark wisp of hair.

"It is a boy," said Father, his smile even wider. "We have decided to call him Elijah."

"Yijah," repeated Cynthia softly.

It was the name of one of our uncles, a name from the Bible, a big and joyful name, I thought. This baby was going to have to do a lot of growing to fit into it.

His little hands waved jerkily in the air. His eyes looked everywhere, as if wondering where he was and who we were.

Something inside me melted like a chunk of butter. I am your big sister, I thought. I am going to take care of you. I reached out one finger to touch him. And, amazingly, the baby closed his tiny fist around it.

All that day we remained in camp so Mother could rest. Mrs. McReynolds came to our wagon several times to help care for her and the baby. Cynthia was fussy, saying that her mouth hurt, but I thought it was more likely she was just missing Mother. Louvina and I tried to distract her with songs and games, and later John took her for a little ride on Polly. Meanwhile Father did some of the washing and all of the cooking.

He boiled up an old sage hen that John had shot, cooking it most of the day. The steam rising up out of the pot smelled so appetizing that I could hardly wait for supper. But when mealtime finally came, I was disappointed to find that the meat was tough. The soup was good, though. Father took some to Jesse Clark, who was so sick now that he could not eat it. Mother had a little with her tea and toast. The rest of us finished it, and wished we had more.

That evening after supper Father read to us the story of Elijah from the Bible. The night was warm and clear. The last coals of the campfire glowed red in the dark.

Overhead the sky was filled with a million stars. They were our blanket, I thought, like Grandma's quilt spread over me, close and comforting.

Father's voice was clear and strong, as if he might still be smiling in the dark. He read about the prophet Elijah: how he was fed miraculously by ravens, how he cured a sick boy, how he overcame his enemies and brought rain to a land stricken by drought, all with the help of God.

"Oh," I couldn't help saying out loud, "if only the ravens would fly down and feed us!"

Father reached out and squeezed my hand.

Then from the wagon I heard again that tiny birdlike cry that I had first heard that morning. And I felt a flood of hope.

So many bad things had happened to us along our way: storms and Indians and terrible sickness and death. Still, it seemed as if someone was watching over us from up there among the stars. With the help of God we were going to be all right.

We had to be. We had Elijah now.

Fourteen

"What do you think of our moving on today?" I heard Father asking in a low voice as I opened my eyes the next morning.

I couldn't quite make out Mother's reply.

"You know I would rather not," Father went on, "but it is already the end of September. We are a whole month later than we planned. And at Fort Hall they warned of snowstorms beginning in October in the mountains."

For a moment there was silence.

Then Mother answered in a small but firm voice, "The baby and I can ride as well on this featherbed as not."

So that morning after breakfast we moved on again. Father traveled slowly, so as not to jolt the wagon too much, and stopped often to make sure that Mother and little Elijah were all right. Mother's face was still tired and ghostly pale. But the baby slept as sweetly as if he were being rocked in a downy cradle.

Jesse Clark remained very sick. John drove his wagon

now, while Rebecca, the oldest of the McReynolds children, herded their few loose cattle.

A few days after that we reached the Columbia River. We came upon it just at dusk, after a hard day of travel through dry and dusty hills. I stood on the river's sandy banks, where not a tree nor a blade of grass grew, and looked out over its rushing gray-blue water. I was amazed at how wide and powerful it was, and grateful that we would not have to cross it. Surely, I thought, we must be almost to the end of our journey. For this was the river Father had talked about in those long-ago days when he had first dreamed of going to Oregon.

"Yes," he agreed, with a trace of a tired smile, when I asked him. "We still have a few more mountains to cross. Difficult ones. But it won't be so long now."

Jesse Clark would not cross that last range of mountains. He died that night. Once more from inside the wagon I heard the sounds of low mournful singing. When I asked Father what funeral hymn they sang, he told me, "There Is a Land of Pure Delight." I nodded. Somehow it comforted me to think that Jesse was with his mother and father now in that promised land.

The next day the Clark wagon was left behind, the three remaining Clarks riding with Mrs. McReynolds and her children.

Wearily, ploddingly, we pushed on. And still our troubles were not over. Sometimes I thought I was trapped in some strange and terrible nightmare, and no matter how many times I pinched myself, I could never wake up. Because now it was Father who was taken sick. For several days he had been feverish, but he refused to give in to it. He dragged along, driving the team, building the fires, taking care of Mother and the baby. But finally one after-noon after making camp, he could do no more. He fell into bed, groaning with fever.

That evening John had to do everything, even the cook-ing. He put up the tent for Father to sleep in, took care of the animals, did the milking, then prepared a supper for us of fried bacon and mush.

I looked down at that plate of the same old food, hidden under a dark puddle of molasses. I was so tired of it. As I picked up my spoon, somehow the thought of a potato crept into my mind. I was so hungry that I could eat a whole peck of them. And not even cooked, just raw. Or that cabbage from the Indians' garden. I could still see it inside my head, round and plump and deep green.

"My kingdom for a cabbage," I sighed to myself as I scraped the last spoonful of mush from my tin plate.

Mother must have been having the same thoughts. Later that night, after John finally returned from taking care of the animals, I heard her talking to him from her bed in the wagon.

"I am so hungry, John," she said. "Can't you get me something more to eat?"

"I'll try to cook up some corn bread in the frying pan," he answered.

A few minutes later she sighed gratefully.

"Thank you, John. That tastes so good."

When I got up the next morning and saw what was left in the frying pan, I was amazed. That corn bread was only half-cooked. Mother must have been awfully hungry to think it tasted good.

At any other time John and I would have had a good laugh about it. This morning, though, there seemed nothing to laugh at. The day was cold and raw, the sky a heavy gray. I shivered as I walked around, gathering sticks for the fire. We had to finish the corn bread for breakfast, as there was nothing else. Cynthia refused to eat it.

"Don't yike it!" she whimpered. "No good."

Worst of all, Father was no better. He lay in bed inside the tent—the same tent where Louvina had lain when she was so sick, I couldn't help remembering—muttering and moaning with the fever. I took him a cup of tea, but he pushed it away, hardly seeming to recognize me.

What were we going to do? I wondered, as I walked back to the fire. Should we wait for Father to recover, or try to move on? Could we move on? Mother lay in bed in the wagon, still too weak to do anything except take care of the baby. And Mrs. McReynolds had not recovered from the deaths of Captain and Mrs. Clark and Jesse. Though she was strong in body, her mind seemed clouded. She waited mutely for Father to tell her what to do. Last night John had taken all the burden on his thin shoulders. But it was too much for him all alone. I could tell by his bent back and the anxious look in his eyes as he hurried from one chore to another. He too was waiting for Father to tell him what to do.

We all depended on Father. It was his strength that had brought us this far. Now suddenly it was gone.

Just then I heard him cry out again from the tent.

"No!" he groaned, as if he were in agony. "No!"

A shiver of dread ran all the way through me. Could this be the beginning of his delirium? As if I had opened a tightly sealed box, all kinds of terrible thoughts came tumbling out, one on top of another. Captain Clark raving with madness day after day. Mrs. Clark's lonely grave.

Oxen so weak and worn-out that they could not stand, lying helpless on the trail. Dead Indians piled up in tepees. Sad, quiet funeral hymns sung by fewer and fewer people. For the first time in all our long journey, I thought we might not make it after all.

What would we do if Father should die?

I looked up into the sky. Through the gray mist of clouds off to the west, I could make out the dim outline of rugged mountain peaks. Father had told me their names: Mount Hood, Mount Jefferson, Mount Saint Helens. And I remembered his words to Mother a few days back: "At Fort Hall they warned of snowstorms beginning in October in the mountains."

All at once I knew what Father would say if he could.

I hurried to find John.

"We have to keep moving," I told him. "I will help."

That day was the hardest of all the hard days of our journey. John drove the wagon. Father lay in back, still tossing and turning and crying out fitfully. Mother sat propped up with pillows in front, Elijah in her arms and Cynthia close by. I herded our loose stock and took care of Father and Mother's needs and found scraps of bread and bacon for lunch, and with Louvina's help, tried to do all the things I had watched Mother doing for these past months.

The oxen, sore-necked and sore-footed and bone-weary, seemed scarcely able to move. Walking along behind the wagon, I concentrated on just putting one foot down in front of the other.

Left foot. Right foot. One step closer to Oregon. Another step closer to Oregon. Now do it again. Left foot. Right foot . . .

Into my tired brain crept a picture of Grandma. It seemed as if I could see her a long time ago, a little bit of a thing trudging along beside her young husband through the dense forests, across wide rivers and icy streams, into the lonely wilderness that was Indiana. Maybe she had felt then something like I felt now. Not really brave. Probably it took a long time to become brave, and I was still full of fears. But just doing what had to be done. Facing west and putting one foot in front of the other. Not giving up. Making it through. Enduring.

We made only four or five miles that day. Still, I told myself, it was four or five miles closer to where we were going.

That evening, while John did the milking, I managed to cook up some cornmeal mush for supper. I took a plate to Mother, and she smiled when she saw it.

"You did this, Mary Ellen?" she said softly. "You must have been watching me more carefully than I thought." Then her eyes filled with tears. "You have done so much today to help. I don't know how we would have managed without you."

I could feel myself standing straighter and taller as I went to the tent to give Father his cup of tea. This time he was able to drink it. Though his face was flushed, which meant he still had fever, he seemed a little better.

"Thank you," he whispered, trying to smile.

Father passed the night peacefully. And the next morning he seemed better again. John and I looked at each other, and in his eyes I saw the relief I felt. The worst was over, I thought. Father's fever had broken.

Every day after that, Father slowly improved. Soon he was sitting up and once more telling John what to do. A few days after that he was able to drive the team, sitting up on the spring seat. It was good to see him there, even if he was not his usual cheerful self. He was so quiet, and looked so very weary.

And so we managed to drag ourselves along until we reached The Dalles. This was a small trading post located at a notch in the high hills that ran along the Columbia River. It looked like a jumping-off place, with nowhere to jump but into the river. There was a Methodist mission there, a few tumbledown cabins and tents, a handful of Frenchmen with Indian wives, and that was all.

All the same, The Dalles was a busy place. Two dozen or more families were camped there, their wagons and tents fanned out on the flat ground. Children were running around, most without shoes, while the women visited and rested, did the washing, and tried to cook some different meals with rice from the trading post and fish they had bought from the Indians. A hospital was set up in one tent, and it was filled with the sick. The men were busy taking apart wagons and repairing them, and planning what came next. For here, Father had told us, every traveler had to make a choice. Some would continue the journey by wagon over the rugged Cascade Mountains, while others floated the rest of the way by boat or raft down the Columbia River.

Father had decided long ago that we would try to cross over the mountains. We thought Mrs. McReynolds would come with us. But while we were camped at The Dalles, she met a family from the town next to hers back in Ohio. They were planning to go the rest of the way by flatboat, and she decided to join them.

"Are you sure?" Father asked, looking at her with concern. "You know you are welcome to come with us."

Something seemed to have come over Mrs. McReynolds in the last few days, I thought. It was as if she had awakened from a long sleep. In those eyes that had been so dull, I saw a new spark of life.

"I am sure," she replied firmly.

Louvina and I went down to the river to watch as her wagon and two others were taken apart, then loaded piece by piece onto flatboats. On the bottom of the boat went the running gear. Next came the wagon beds, with their covers removed. On top of this were piled all the remaining food and provisions. And finally would come the passengers, packed in tight like sardines in a box.

Early the next morning, as they loaded the last of their belongings on board, we said good-bye to Mrs. McReynolds and the eight children. They were many sizes, from tall, sturdy, pink-cheeked Rebecca down to sad-eyed little Willie, with fair hair and dark, but all one family now.

This parting was the hardest of all. Our families had shared so much sorrow and joy, and had helped each other through the most difficult times. Mrs. McReynolds's face was flushed with feeling, and she held tight to Willie's hand as she thanked Father and Mother for their help.

"If you had not stayed with us, we would never have made it to this place," she said simply.

Mother was too overcome to speak. But Father answered quietly, "We wish you Godspeed."

We waved good-bye, as the heavily loaded boats moved precariously out onto the rushing river. It was strange, I thought. Even as we had started our journey alone, it seemed that we were going to finish it the same way.

Then slowly we walked back to our wagon to prepare to cross those last mountains.

Fifteen

It rose up in front of us: the highest, grandest mountain that I had ever seen. Cone-shaped and fringed at the bottom with dark evergreens and the shimmering gold leaves of autumn, it changed to bare gray rock as you looked up toward the peak. And at the very top, almost covered by little puffs of cloud, was a neat white cap of snow.

"That is Mount Hood," Father told us.

We would not have to cross over it, he said, only go around its side on a trail called the Barlow Road.

To me it seemed too hard a task. Our oxen were just bones covered by too-large skin, with hardly a spark of life left in them. Rover limped or walked on three legs most of the time. The wagon cover, once so white that it dazzled my eyes, was now a brownish-gray, torn and mud-stained. As for us, our clothes were patched and worn through. If it hadn't been for Mother's motto of "A stitch in time saves nine," we all would have been in rags and walking barefoot, like so many others we saw.

My blue, flower-sprigged dress had been mended so many times that it looked like patchwork, and the flowers had faded completely away. The wood splints showed through our threadbare sunbonnets. My shoes were almost out at the toes. And Father's and John's breeches had patches on top of patches.

Most of all we were just so weary of traveling. But it had to be done. Wash the dishes. Pack up the kettle and the frying pan. Shake out the bedding, roll it up, and stow it inside the wagon. Hitch up the team. Crack the whip. Listen to the wagon wheels creak, as if complaining, then slowly start to turn. Another day on the endless trail. It was all I could remember, and all I knew how to do.

Over hills and hollows we crept along, always in the shadow of that great mountain. There were more streams to cross, and another river. This one, a branch of the Deschutes, was not very wide but deep and swift. The oxen refused to go into it.

Never, not even back in Kansas, had they seen water as fast-moving as this. The animals would start up, but as soon as they reached the rushing water, they stopped abruptly. The poor things couldn't get up the courage to make the plunge.

"Ho-ay! Ho-ay!" shouted Father.

He coaxed and goaded and finally, in frustration, gave them the whip. But nothing worked. They couldn't seem to overcome their fear.

Just downstream was a little ferryboat.

"You and the children will have to cross by ferry with the wagon," Father told Mother, his face grim but determined. "John and I are going to make these oxen swim."

Father paid two Indians a dollar to take us across. The wagon was unhitched and rolled onto the flatboat, and we floated easily to the other side. Then, as Louvina and I stood watching on the bank, Father and John again tried to force the stubborn oxen into the water. It was a long, hard struggle, but at last they managed to get them swimming. And soon we were all on the other side of the river.

We were now in the Cascade Mountains. Like the Blues before them, they were rocky, and in places even steeper and higher. The trees were giant pines and cedars and firs, so tall that it hurt my neck to try to see the tops of them and so close together that they blocked out the sun. The road was rough and hard to follow. Up and down it went, over sharp rocks, through mudholes, twisting and turning around stumps and tree roots and fallen logs.

"This must be the worst road ever devised," sighed Mother, after we had been struggling for hours and getting nowhere.

The oxen strained and pulled with all their waning strength. The wagon lurched and bounced. In the worst places we all had to get out and walk, Mother and Louvina holding Cynthia by the hand and me carrying little Elijah. Through the paper-thin soles of my shoes I could feel every stone that I stepped on. But I didn't think of my sore feet. I held the warm sleeping baby close to my chest, feeling proud that Mother trusted me to carry him. And I made very sure that I did not stumble.

On the third day we came to a place called Laurel Hill.

"Whoa!" called Father to the oxen. As they creaked to a stop, he walked ahead to look it over.

I stood next to him, looking down, unable to believe that the road really went over this steep drop. It was almost perpendicular and about half a mile long, narrow and winding, rocky and muddy and slippery. It reminded me of a very tall, crooked chimney.

"What are we going to do?" I asked Father anxiously.

He didn't answer right away. Instead he walked around, examining the nearby trees and rocks, testing the slippery slope.

"Others have done it," he said finally, "and so will we. Do you see the bark rubbed off the large trees here at the top? Some have chained their wagons to a tree, then let out the chain little by little. Others probably cut down small trees and tied them on in back to break their descent, or piled rocks in front of the wagon wheels."

After thinking it over for a while, Father decided not only to use chains but to drag a small tree besides. First he unhitched all of the oxen except Buck and Ben. The other animals would be led down the hill later. He had John cut down a little tree with many branches and tie it to the back of the wagon. Then he attached a chain to the rear axle and wrapped the other end around a strong standing tree at the top of the hill. He set the wagon brake on the last notch.

Mother sat watching on a tree stump, Elijah in her arms, the rest of us nearby.

"Gee, Buck!" ordered Father. "Gee, Ben!"

Very slowly they started down the hill. The locked wheels made a dismal screeching sound that echoed through the mountains.

From up above Father let out the chain a little bit at a time. John walked alongside Buck, one hand gripping his horn, holding him back. The oxen slid from side to side, pushed by the tongue of the wagon. In spite of Father and John's efforts I could see them beginning to pick up speed.

"Oh no!" Mother cried softly.

The heavy wagon clattering behind them shoved the oxen along. Faster and faster they went. I took in a deep breath and forgot to let it out, watching helplessly.

John was still clinging to Buck's horn, but he couldn't hold him back any longer. His hat went flying off. His feet skidded over the muddy ground. He was going to be trampled. Jump! I thought. As if he had heard me, John finally gave up and leapt out of the way.

As they neared the bottom of the hill, the oxen were going at a full gallop. It looked as if the wagon would run right over them. I waited for the crash, the sickening splintering of wood, the overturned broken wagon that would be the final disaster.

Then, miraculously, they were down. John came sliding along behind the wagon, picking up his hat and dusting off his breeches.

"Hurrah for our team!" he cheered in his loud, piercing voice.

"Thank goodness," breathed Mother, and Cynthia clapped her hands, laughing. Another obstacle had been overcome.

But some time during that night, while we were sleeping, poor old Buck died. The next morning we all gathered around his body, looking down in sorrow.

"I don't know what happened," Father said, sadly shaking his head. "Maybe he was injured somehow coming down Laurel Hill."

Or maybe, I thought, he had just finally worn out after bringing us so far. And I was glad that he had gotten away with that bread dough back in the Blue Mountains.

Father hitched up Bright in Buck's place, and put a cow that Mrs. McReynolds had left us in Bright's place, and we went on again.

All along our way through the mountains we kept seeing abandoned wagons and yokes and chains, as well as dead oxen and mules. It looked as if many families had been forced to travel the last miles of their journey on foot. One morning, just as we were starting out, we came upon three good wagons standing deserted at the side of the trail.

Father stopped our wagon, and we went to look inside. Most of the contents were still there. I saw trunks of clothes, pots, dishes, all sorts of useful things.

"Take anything you need," Father said to Mother.

"Oh no!" she objected. "I couldn't do that. It wouldn't be right."

Father put his hand on her shoulder. "It's all right, Angelina," he insisted gently. "The owners will not be coming back. The only ones to benefit will be the Indians. And they will take what they want and likely burn the rest."

Mother's face looked torn. But finally she mustered up the courage to take a few things that we really needed: a warm coat for Father, a flatiron, a coffee pot, a camp kettle, a washboard to replace the one that Polly had kicked to pieces, and a pretty brass candlestick.

Later that day, just as Father had predicted, we saw a band of Indians heading in the direction of those wagons.

"Oh dear," sighed Mother with a regretful little smile, "I guess we should have taken more."

On we went through the mountains, crossing and re-crossing yet another river, sloshing through icy streams, climbing up and down steep and muddy hills. It was cold, the kind of damp cold that pierced through my clothing to chill me right down to the bones. But we had no snow. Most days the weather was drizzly and rainy. Luckily we had all that wood around us now, so we could have good warm fires in the evenings.

On the tenth day after we had left The Dalles, at about noon, I was walking next to the wagon, gazing down at my shoes and wondering how long it would be before my toes poked all the way through. I looked up, and suddenly, through the tall trees ahead, I caught a glimpse of what seemed to be a wide, open valley. I blinked. Was this some sort of vision? I wondered. Or could it be real? Looking again, I saw that the valley was grassy and sprinkled with spreading oak trees and fringed around the edges with blue-green firs that seemed to reach up into the mountains, into the blue sky above.

Yes, I thought. This was the Oregon we had been hoping to find.

Father had seen it too. He halted the team. Coming back to the wagon, he looked up at Mother sitting on the spring seat.

"Praise the Lord!" he said. "We are through at last." A great weight seemed to have lifted off his shoulders, and he was smiling the way he used to back home.

Mother stared ahead, her face perfectly still, her eyes bright. I saw her mouth move, but no words came out.

"Oh good," said Louvina, smiling happily. "Now we can play in our yard and go to meeting."

Just then John came riding up with the cattle. Seeing us stopped, he looked to see what was wrong. Then he too gazed out over the beautiful valley below.

"Hip! Hip! Hurrah for Oregon!" he shouted, and he tossed his hat so high in the air that I didn't see it come down.

Cynthia was looking up at him with a puzzled expression on her face.

"What is it—O'gen?" she asked.

And we all laughed with joy.

We came down out of the mountains into that valley and found farms and food. Father bought a few vegetables, and I was able once again to taste something green. In four more days we made our way to a place called Howell's Prairie, where the land was flat and ringed with mountains, and the soil looked rich. Here we made camp.

It was October sixteenth, and we had been on our way for more than six long months.

That evening, sitting in a warm, close circle around the campfire, Father read to us a psalm of thanksgiving, Psalm 107.

"Oh give thanks unto the Lord, for he is good," it began. And the psalm went on to tell how the Lord delivered his people out of the wilderness and saved the hungry and thirsty who cried out to him. Later, Father came to a verse that said, ". . . so he bringeth them unto their desired haven." It seemed to me that those words had been written just for us.

After he finished reading, Father closed the Bible, and for a moment everyone was silent.

Then he turned to Mother, his face in the firelight looking younger than it had in a long time.

"Can you tell us what you are most thankful for?" he asked.

Mother's answer came quickly, her voice quiet and sober. "I am thankful that we all got through alive."

Father nodded, smiling. Then he looked across at me. "And you, Mary Ellen?"

There were so many things, I thought, staring into the little red, licking flames. But one stood out in my mind.

"I am thankful that you were not sick very long," I said. "And John was never sick at all."

"I am thankful that Blackie gave us milk all the way through," piped up Louvina.

"I am thankful that I got to come with you," added John.

Father looked down at Cynthia, leaning sleepily on his knee.

"And what about you, little mite?" he asked. "What are you thankful for?"

"Yijah!" said Cynthia.

After that we all bowed our heads and Father said a prayer, thanking God for delivering us from the wilderness and bringing us to this beautiful land of promise.

Sixteen

Father rented forty acres of land. He mortgaged one pair of our oxen for seed grain, and sold Bright for thirty dollars to buy some of the supplies we needed. On the land was a one-room log cabin with a stone fireplace for cooking and a storeroom at the north end. We set up our tent nearby and went to work fixing it up.

The first thing Father did was to make rockers for the padded box that first Cynthia and then Elijah had slept in during our journey.

"Now you have a real cradle," I told him, as Mother placed Elijah in it for the first time.

He lay there looking up at us, kicking and cooing and smiling. He was such a happy baby. It seemed to me that his bright, dark eyes were staring straight into mine. He knows me, I thought. And I wondered if, young as he was, Elijah remembered that I was the one who had carried him over those last rough, steep parts of the trail.

I reached out my hand and gently rocked the cradle until his eyes fluttered closed.

Next Father built a table, some rough stools to sit on, and bedsteads for all of us. The bedsteads were made from young trees trimmed down into poles and fastened to the walls. On shelves underneath the frames he piled fragrant fir branches. On top of those went the feather ticks we had carried all the way across the plains, and on top of the ticks our goosedown pillows and bright-colored quilts. It felt good finally to sleep in a real bed again.

In the meantime Mother and I were busy papering goods boxes to use as cupboards and dressers. One morning I took every one of our cooking utensils and the big brass kettle down to a nearby spring. There, with ashes, sand, and soap, I did my best to scour away all the signs of our long journey. The next day we unpacked everything from the wagon and set it in place. On crude shelves built into the wall went the two remaining blue-and-white cups from her mother's china that Mother had refused to part with on the trail, the small, cracked looking glass that Father used for shaving, our few books, Father's Bible, and a faded tintype picture of Grandma with all of her living children.

"There," said Mother, looking pleased with her efforts. "Now we are at home."

Seeing the picture reminded me that our folks back in Arkansas did not know we had arrived safely in Oregon.

"May I write a letter to Grandma?" I asked.

"Of course," said Mother. She wrote a letter home and let me put mine with it:

Dear Grandma,

It is with pleasure that I take up my pen to write you a few lines. We are all well at present. I have seen many curiosities since I last saw you. Parts of the journey I liked very much, but some were tiresome. There was a great deal of sickness, and parts of the road were almost impossible to travel. I am sorry to tell you that Daisy was drowned on the Kaw River and Lillie died from eating a poison weed. We arrived on the sixteenth of October, making our journey six months long.

I like Oregon very well, what I have seen of it, but it does not yet seem like home. I cannot be running over to Grandma's house like I used to do. We have neighbors but no meetinghouse and no schoolhouse. Father will teach us this winter. There is talk of building a schoolhouse in the spring.

You should see Elijah. He is a good baby and hardly cries except when he is hungry. Louvina and I have the thimbles you gave us, and we are sewing on our quilts. I now have fourteen squares.

We have your likeness, and it does us all a great deal of good to look at it. I have written everything I can think of, so I had better close. Give my love to Uncle Jimmie and Cousin Will and Great-aunt Harriet and all the rest, and write soon.

Yours affectionately,
Mary Ellen Todd

As soon as I finished writing, I realized that I had said nothing about Grandma coming to be with us in Oregon. And I knew the reason that I hadn't. The feeling had been coming over me for a long time. The chances were that Grandma would not be able to make that long, hard journey. Once she could have. I could imagine her as a young woman striding over those plains and rivers and mountains as easily as if she were stepping on clouds. But she was old now, and not so strong. Probably, I thought, we would never see Grandma again.

I felt a pang of loneliness then, so sharp that it was like a deep-down ache in my insides. An ache that might never go away. My eyes were stinging with tears as I folded the letter to give to Mother.

As soon as the cabin was roughly furnished, Father and John put in a crop. To tide us over until harvesting time Father got some extra work splitting rails for fences, and John went to work on a neighboring farm, coming home only on Sundays. But even this might not be enough to get us through the winter, Father said. So Mother bought a spinning wheel. She and Louvina and I spun wool into yarn and then knitted the yarn into socks, which Mother found she could sell at a good price. Every evening, sitting around the stone fireplace, Louvina and I had to knit one inch.

Father was not used to splitting rails, and one day he injured both of his hands. Bruises turned into abscesses, and for several weeks he could not do any work. While we were sorry to see him suffer, I enjoyed having the chance to wait on him. Louvina and I fed him, tied his shoes, combed his hair for him, and turned the pages of his book.

"I don't know what I would do without you children," he said, smiling.

"Why do you have to split rails?" I asked him. "Couldn't you make pottery instead, like you used to?"

Father shook his head regretfully. "I have no kiln," he reminded me. "And even if I did, very few of the people settling hereabouts could afford to buy my wares. No, we have come to a place where the land is rich. We must put all of our strength into farming now."

Father had been able to buy half a side of beef and a few vegetables, so we would not go hungry that winter. Still, I kept longing for more vegetables. John was always teasing me about my "mountain fever appetite." One day, while poking through some dense, high weeds, I discovered a little patch of forgotten potatoes on our neighbor's land.

"Can I dig them up?" I asked Father.

"You will have to ask Mr. McCorkle," he replied. "Perhaps he will let you do it on shares."

So I mustered up my courage and went to talk to him.

Mr. McCorkle looked at me, shrewd blue eyes peering out of his round, white-whiskered face.

"On shares, you say?" he repeated, frowning doubtfully. "Half for your family and half for me?"

I nodded.

Suddenly he thrust out his hand. "All right, young lady," he agreed. "You have a deal."

Louvina and I went to work. It was difficult hunting for the dried-up vines among all those tall weeds, and then digging the small potatoes out of the ground. Winter was fast approaching, and the cold made our fingers sting. Sometimes Louvina cried, her hands ached so much. We took to making fires, working a while, then stopping to warm ourselves around the small blaze.

We kept at it, day after day, until at last we had six sacks of potatoes for ourselves and six for Mr. McCorkle.

When I brought them to show Mother, her face broke into one of her rare smiles.

"I am proud of you, Mary Ellen," she told me. "You stuck to the task until it was done."

"It must have been that mountain appetite that made you dig so hard," Father added, laughing. "You two shall have new books for this."

"And, come spring, new dresses," promised Mother.

I felt warm inside, almost as if I were standing close by the fire. Mother did care for me. I could feel it, even if she was never going to show it with hugs and kisses the way Grandma did. Then suddenly I realized something else. It had been weeks now since I had thought about my real mother. That picture of her that I had carried around so long in my head seemed to have slipped away. And somehow, without my even noticing it, Mother had taken her place.

Time passed, and now it was truly winter. We rejoiced that we had our snug little cabin, enough food to eat, good warm fires, and books to read. Polly and Blackie and the other remaining cattle rested and fed in rich pastures, and Rover was his old self again, happily chasing squirrels.

Sometimes on warm days Louvina and I still played in our covered wagon, which now stood empty near the cabin. One day, sitting up on the spring seat, I picked up Father's whip again. Once more I tried to crack it the way he did. And once more I couldn't do it. Still, it seemed to me that it didn't feel quite so heavy.

Every day after that, while Louvina played her pretend games with our dolls inside the wagon, I practiced lifting the big whip, holding it over the heads of an imaginary team of oxen, flicking my wrist hard.

And finally, one day, I heard a faint, "Pop!"

"You did it!" exclaimed Louvina, poking her brown head out of the wagon. "You made it crack."

"Yes," I said happily.

A few days later, as I was approaching the cabin door carrying the water bucket, I overheard Father and Mother talking.

"Did you know," said Father, "that Mary Ellen is beginning to be able to crack the whip?"

Pride welled up inside me and brimmed over in a smile. But then I heard Mother's reply.

"I'm afraid it is not a very ladylike thing to do," she said.

There it was again, that constant concern about being a lady. Mother would always be pushing it at me, it seemed. And I would always be resisting. But in spite of her words I walked around for the next few days filled with a secret joy. I had the power to set things going.

It was December now, and the days were drawing near to Christmas. To get ready for our first celebration in our new home, Mother cleaned the cabin from top to bottom. Louvina and I went out into the woods and gathered ferns and vines and evergreen branches. Arranging them in bunches, we decorated the walls and shelves and table. Then we helped Mother make six real candles.

She had borrowed the candle molds from Mrs. Daugherty, another of our neighbors. In the center of each mold we carefully placed a cotton wick. After that we poured in hot tallow and let it cool. When the tallow was set, we warmed the molds just a little. And out came six nice, straight, white candles.

On Christmas morning I was the first to wake up. For a moment I just lay there beneath my two warm quilts, breathing in the sweet piney smell of evergreens. Then, opening my eyes, I looked around at the looping chains of evergreens hanging from the shelves, the pickle jar filled with ferns on the table, and next to it the beautiful brass candlestick with its tall white candle waiting to be lighted.

I nudged Louvina, sleeping next to me.

"Christmas gift!" I whispered in her ear.

It was a game we played in our family every Christmas morning. The one who said this greeting first scored a point.

In a moment Louvina was jumping out of bed and whispering in Cynthia's ear, "Christmas gift!" And soon everyone was up, greeting each other and laughing. "Christmas gift! Christmas gift!"

We did not expect any real gifts this year. But Mother surprised Louvina and me with mittens that she had knitted for us late in the evenings after we were asleep. And Father had carved a doll with a wooden head, and Mother had dressed it in scraps of red-and-white fabric for Cynthia. So now she had a doll just like ours. And for baby Elijah there was a string of buttons to play with.

"I yike her!" Cynthia kept squealing with excitement, her pudgy fingers holding her new doll tight.

At noon we sat down to our Christmas dinner. The table was covered with tasty dishes: roast beef and gravy, mashed potatoes, cabbage slaw, corn bread baked in our Dutch oven, and sweet butter to go with it. Mother had also made some pumpkin butter, which added a spicy flavor. With all this and Mother's sweet cake, and some stick candy that John had brought us, we were as full as we could be.

After dinner we sang hymns and carols for a while. Then Father brought out his chessboard, and he and John settled in for a game, while Mother and I tried to teach Louvina to play checkers. Later the three of us children went outside and played hide-and-seek and Annie Over and Pussy Wants a Corner. We played until Cynthia stubbed her toe and started to cry, and then we all went back inside.

Finally the evening chores were done. The cows had been milked and all the animals fed. It was time to light our Christmas candles.

One by one Father put a match to them, and the cabin was filled with a warm, flickering glow.

"Ohhh!" breathed Cynthia, her eyes wide.

We gathered around the stone fireplace, Father and Mother in the two splint-bottomed easy chairs, the rest of us on the floor. Father cracked hazelnuts, while Mother set some corn to popping in the Dutch oven. Looking into the flames, seeing the old familiar chairs drawn up by the fire, smelling the warm smell of popcorn, I thought that our cabin was beginning to feel like home.

"Remember the time we tried to pop corn out in the rain near the Kaw River?" John asked, grinning.

"It was all hard and tasted like smoke," I recalled. "But we thought it was good." Then I remembered something else. "And how about our two-year-old yearling that was drowned in the crossing?"

John's face flushed pink. But then he retorted by singing, "Enter into my jaw and sit down on my throat," and I had to laugh.

After a few minutes Mother settled back in her easy chair. Her face seemed to have filled out and become softer in the last few weeks. "I wonder what it is like now out on the plains," she said.

"In many places the snow could be several feet deep

and the temperature well below zero," Father answered. "I wouldn't want to be stranded out there in the middle of winter."

I thought about the constant wind out on the plains, how fierce and icy it would be now. I thought about blowing snow and howling wolves. And in spite of the cheerful warmth of our fire, I felt myself shiver.

"I hope all of the wagon trains got through all right," I said.

Mother seemed far away, thinking of something. "I keep wondering about the Grants," she said softly.

We talked about the Grants and brave Mrs. Mc-Reynolds with her brood of children and the Tedroses and Sarah Jane's family. I thought of the mule train with the words "Sure and Swift" painted on its wagon cover that had kept passing us, and the frightened family that had turned back because of cholera on the Platte River. What were they all doing now?

That reminded me again of Grandma and our other relatives back in Arkansas.

"Do you think they have our letters now and know we are safe?" I asked.

"I hope so," answered Mother. "And soon we will have a letter from them."

I would keep on writing to Grandma. I would tell her all about our first Christmas and how Elijah could roll over now and might be getting his first tooth. I would tell her about the books that Father had borrowed from Mr. McCorkle and the latest plans for building a school-house. Even if she could not come to live with us in Oregon, we could stay close to each other by letter.

Then all at once I had a wonderful idea. I would take

my nine-patch squares that Grandma had started me on and I would sew them into a quilt for Elijah. I had enough, almost, for a baby quilt. It would be a special gift to him from me, but it would also be a gift from Grandma. Another way of remembering her.

I couldn't help smiling at the thought. Then Father took down his Bible from the shelf, and we all drew close together while he read the story of the first Christmas.

"And the angel said unto them, 'Fear not: for, behold, I bring you good tidings of great joy, which shall be to all people. For unto you is born this day in the city of David a Savior, which is Christ the Lord. And this shall be a sign unto you; ye shall find the babe wrapped in swaddling clothes, lying in a manger.' "

I looked at our baby Elijah, sleeping peacefully now in his cradle next to the fireplace. Cynthia had fallen asleep too, in Mother's arms, still clutching her new doll close to her. Louvina was beginning to yawn.

It was time for bed. Sleepily Louvina and I crawled under our quilts. Mother tucked them snugly around us.

"Good night," came her quiet voice.

I felt something touch my hair, as light and soft as a whisper, or maybe an angel's wing. Was it Mother's hand? It was gone so quickly that I could not be sure.

Then Father blew out the candle, and everything was still.

Author's Note

Most of this story is true. There really was a Mary Ellen Todd, who traveled with her family on the Oregon Trail when she was nine years old. After Mary Ellen grew up, she liked to tell stories about this memorable journey, first to her own daughter, Adrietta, and later to her grandchildren. When Adrietta Applegate Hixon was an old woman, she wrote down her mother's stories. And finally, after her death, they were published in a little book called *On to Oregon! A True Story of a Young Girl's Journey Into the West*. It is on this book that my story is based.

I stumbled upon Mary Ellen Todd's account while doing research about the Oregon Trail. Thousands of travelers moved along this trail during the years of westward migration, from 1840 to 1870, and many of them wrote about their experiences in diaries and letters to relatives back home. However, nearly all of these were adults. It was difficult to learn what the journey had been like for children. A few reminiscences existed, memories written down years later by men and women who had made the trip as children, but in most cases their recollections were sketchy. *On to Oregon!* was different. It was filled with descriptions and vivid details. The language and writing style would probably seem old-fashioned to modern readers. But, reading it, I immediately felt as if I been along on the journey with this young girl and her family. I wanted others to share that journey, and so I decided to retell Mary Ellen's story.

In the retelling I have not changed any of the major events of the story. The Todd family had to deal with most of the problems commonly faced along the trail: disagreements among members of a wagon train, dangerous river crossings, illness, injuries, shortages of food and water, loss of livestock. They also had difficulties worse than many. Traveling in 1852, one of the worst years of the cholera epidemic, they nearly lost a daughter to this terrible disease. They experienced an attack by hostile Indians, something that travelers commonly feared but which rarely actually happened. Through all of their troubles Mary Ellen's family reacted with a mixture of common sense, courage, and religious faith that was typical of these westward-moving pioneers.

Much was left out of Mary Ellen's recollections, and this I have had to imagine. Names of relatives and friends were invented, as were some of Mary Ellen's feelings, in particular about her grandmother and her biological mother. The Todds' home in Arkansas and their final destination in Oregon have been imagined with the help of historical research. Details of places along the trail have been reconstructed from the first-hand observations of other travelers of the period, as recorded in dozens of their diaries. In addition, I have walked along the Barlow Road under the shadow of towering Mount Hood, and gazed up at the steep cliff called Laurel Hill. I managed to locate the place near Salem that was once called Howell's Prairie, where the Todds first settled. There is still a Howell's Prairie Road, and the area remains a beautiful farming valley.

An interesting sidelight of the westward migration was that it took place less than a decade before the Civil War, during a time of increasing national conflict over the issue of slavery. Some who moved west did so to escape the practice. The Todd family was concerned about this issue, as demonstrated by discussions among the men at one point along the way. Abbott L. Todd, Mary Ellen's father, was a first cousin of Mary Todd, the wife of Abraham Lincoln. A deeply religious man, he was firmly against slavery. But some took the other side. In the book I have reproduced the argument as Mary Ellen recollected it. Though the language is offensive, this is the way the debate sounded at the time.

A few words about the Todd family after the Christmas of 1852, when my story ends: Sometime the following spring Mary Ellen's father came across a newspaper account of a wagon train that had been stranded all winter near Fort Boise. The people were starving, and many had died. Those who survived were forced to slaughter their mules for food, and even to gnaw on their harnesses. On the wagon covers, the rescuers said, could still be seen the painted words, "Sure and Swift." This was the fast-moving and elegant mule train that Mary Ellen had so envied.

According to Mary Ellen's account her father later became an ordained minister, as did Joab Powell, the captain of the large wagon train that had rescued the Todds and Grants from the Indians. The two men met often at religious meetings and became close friends. Mary Ellen grew up in Oregon and married John Applegate, a cattle rancher. Eventually she and her family moved to southwestern Idaho, near the city of Weiser, only a few miles from the Snake River and the trail she had traveled years before. Mary Ellen Todd died in 1924, at the age of eighty-one.

Acknowledgments

I am indebted to a great many sources for help with the research for this book. Although the publications that I read are too numerous to list, books that proved especially valuable were: *Covered Wagon Women: Diaries and Letters from the Western Trails, 1840–1890*, edited by Kenneth L. Holmes; *Conversations with Pioneer Women* by Fred Lockley; *The Great Platte River Road* and *Platte River Road Narratives* by Merrill J. Mattes; and *Women's Diaries of the Westward Journey* by Lillian Schlissel.

In addition I am grateful to many museums, libraries, and historical societies for helping me locate primary source materials and for answering my questions. In Oregon these include the Oregon Historical Society, Lane County Historical Museum, Douglas County Museum, End of the Oregon Trail Interpretive Center in Oregon City, and Oregon Trail Interpretive Center in Baker City. Also helpful were the Bancroft Library at the University of California, Berkeley; The Huntington Library, San Marino, California; National Frontier Trails Center in Independence, Missouri; and the Arkansas Territorial Restoration in Little Rock, Arkansas.

Finally, special thanks to Mary Platt and Paula Peyraud, reference librarians at my own local library in Chappaqua, New York, for their patient assistance in tracking down materials. To Swannee Bennett, Deputy Director and Curator of Collections of the Arkansas Territorial Restoration, for his wonderfully helpful, enthusiastic response to my Arkansas questions. To Nancy Bennett, for sharing with me her mother's recollections of how the game "Annie Over" (also called "Anthony Over" or "Anti-Over") was played. To my good friend Ann Sohn, for her encouragement and many hours of legwork on my behalf in Oregon. And to my husband, Bruce Gavril, for walking the Barlow Road with me.

Most of all, I thank Mary Ellen Todd's daughter, Adrietta, for writing down her mother's memories of the trail in *On to Oregon! A True Story of a Young Girl's Journey Into the West*.